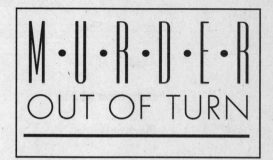

M·U·R·D·E·R
OUT OF TURN

Books by Frances and Richard Lockridge

Hanged for a Sheep

Murder Out of Turn

The Norths Meet Murder

A Pinch of Poison

M·U·R·D·E·R
OUT OF TURN

FRANCES & RICHARD
LOCKRIDGE

HarperPerennial
A Division of HarperCollins*Publishers*

HarperCollins books may be purchased for educational, business, or sales promotional use. For information, please write: Special Markets Department, HarperCollins Publishers, Inc., 10 East 53rd Street, New York, NY 10022.

First HarperPerennial edition published 1994.

Designed by R. Caitlin Daniels

Library of Congress Cataloging-in-Publication Data

Lockridge, Frances Louise Davis.
    Murder out of turn / by Frances and Richard Lockridge.—1st Harper Perennial ed.
        p.   cm.
    "A Mr. and Mrs. North Mystery."
    Previously published: New York : F.A. Stokes, 1940.
    ISBN 0-06-092489-6
    1. Private investigators—New York (State)—Fiction.
I. Lockridge, Richard, 1898–   .   II. Title.
PS3523.0243M79 1994
813' .54—dc20   93-21280

94 95 96 97 98 ❖/RRD 10 9 8 7 6 5 4 3 2 1

With the exception of Pete, the characters in this novel are fictional and have no counterparts in life. Pete is real; the authors work for his keep.

• CONTENTS •

M·U·R·D·E·R
OUT OF TURN

• 1 •

SATURDAY, SEPTEMBER 9:
3:15 P.M. TO 4 P.M.

William Weigand took a hurried look at the sketch map, decided to chance it, and swung left off Route 22 on a narrow macadam road. He drove a few hundred yards and pulled the Buick to the side of the road. He stared at the map and admitted to himself that it had him. Just here, where Mrs. Gerald North had drawn a little wiggly line, there ought to be a side road. But there wasn't any side road. There was only a small and rather pointless brook, which approached the road half-heartedly from the right, dived under it and emerged, not perceptibly refreshed, on the other side.

"Of course," Weigand said to himself, "she could have drawn the brook. Though God knows why. She didn't draw the Croton River."

He back-tracked on the map. Through Brewster on Route 22; that was right, so far. Turn left seven miles out, pass a little wiggly road that might be a brook, bear right at one fork—if it was a fork—and left at another around something marked "White church" and then come to Ireland. That was what it said at the terminus—"Ireland." Mrs. North's maps were as unexpected as Mrs. North, Weigand thought, putting the car back in gear. As one might expect, he thought, leaving the little brook, which might be a road, behind and parting company finally with the assurance which came from the black and white signs which had told him that he was, as he should be, on "N. Y. 22."

There was a fork, which encouraged him, and he bore right. Then there was another, but no church, of any color. Weigand stopped in the middle of the fork and looked around. No church. He sighed and got out and walked back down the road a few yards until he could peer through some low-growing trees on the left. There was something white through the trees, and Weigand climbed halfway up the bank. It was a church, sure enough—not visible from the road, only vaguely white, if you came to that, but certainly a church. Weigand shook his head over Mrs. North, who had risen superior to foliage. He went back to the car and bore left. The road wound and twisted, it went suddenly uphill and even more suddenly down and then it was blocked by a herd of cows. Weigand ground along behind the cows while a small boy nudged them to the side and two farm dogs frightened them back again. Finally he got past and the cows looked at him, mournfully solemn.

He ought to be nearly to "Ireland" now, he thought, as the road turned again on top of a hill. There was a fork which Mrs. North had forgotten, but Weigand, feeling that it was the right fork's turn, took it. He slid cautiously downhill and there, suddenly, was Ireland—"Frank Ireland's Log Cabin. Open All Year." Weigand pulled up and went in to ask about the Norths. Mr. Ireland, a stocky, hoarse man, walked to the door so that he could spit tobacco, beckoned Weigand to follow him and gesticulated by the gas pumps. Weigand should turn left, go about three hundred yards, and find a driveway through the wall on the right. That would be the Norths.

"Pam and Jerry," Mr. Ireland said, unexpectedly. "Tell them I've got cream if they want it." He looked at Weigand. "Great people for cream," he said. It seemed to be a joke. Anyway, Mr. Ireland laughed.

"Thanks," said Weigand. "I'll tell them."

He turned left, drove about a quarter of a mile, and found a gap in the stone wall on the right. He turned in. The Norths' car was pulled halfway up a slope to one side. It was not the car they had that spring, but it was their car, as the license plates told him. He reflected that he was probably the only person in the world who could tell offhand what the Norths' license number was, since neither of the Norths could, and pulled up beside it. Nobody came out of the cabin a little farther up the slope for a moment, and then a large black cat came out.

"Hello, Pete," Weigand said. "How's tricks? How's mice?"

Pete looked at Weigand and came to investigate. He smelled Weigand's shoes and rolled over to be tickled on the belly. Weigand tickled him. Pete scratched playfully, drawing blood. He was, Weigand saw, the same Pete. Weigand left Pete, who spoke indignantly about it, and walked up to the cabin, saying, "Hello!" Nothing happened. He walked around it and found that the land sloped down toward a lake and that near the lake there were two tennis courts and a good many people. That would be Lone Lake; that would be the tournament, which the Norths had assured him he had missed by not coming the weekend before. The tournament, evidently, had waited. He walked down.

There were perhaps twenty people, mostly in tennis shorts or slacks, sitting in canvas chairs along one side, and there were others sitting in linesmen's chairs. Then Weigand heard a familiar voice.

"Damn," said Mrs. North. "Oh, damn!"

A ball rose from Mrs. North's racket on the far side of the court, cleared the backstop and subsided near Weigand. He picked it up and threw it back and both Norths waved their rackets at him.

"Hey," said Mr. North. He said it darkly, as from deep gloom. Weigand raised a hand and went on to a vacant chair. The Norths were playing together and evidently not doing too well.

There was a young woman he had never seen before in the chair next Weigand's.

"Shh!" she said. "Finals. Mixed doubles."

"Right," said Weigand. He watched Mr. North serve, hard to the opposing man. It was a fault. The second was good and went back hard to Mr. North's backhand. It returned, hard, into the net.

"Game," said the umpire, and puzzled over his score-sheet. "The games are five-three, Miss Corbin and Mr. Saunders lead."

Miss Corbin was a slight, dark-eyed girl in shining white tennis shirt and shorts. Her face was clear-etched, in a fashion to make anyone feel, when he looked at her, that his eyes were sharper than he had thought them. Mr. Saunders was a large, blond man in slacks and shirt and bright red sunburn. He went to the net and Miss Corbin served.

"They've each got a set," the girl next Weigand said. "Isn't it exciting?"

Weigand said it was.

"Jerry and Pam looked like taking it," the girl said, "but then Jean and Hardie got going. They've been amazing, the way they played together. They, of all people."

Weigand said he saw. Miss Corbin, who might be either Hardie or Jean, served spitefully to Mrs. North's backhand. Mrs. North lobbed it over Saunders. Miss Corbin covered, but her return arched lazily at the net. Mr. North, coming in, smashed it away and looked pleased. But he snarled angrily when his own return of service went unmolested down the alley and, still unmolested, over the base-line by a yard. Mr. North returned to position, shaking his head angrily. Mrs. North's cross-court on the next service caught the netcord, hung a moment and fell on the Norths' side. Mr. North shook his head darkly, as if he had expected it.

"Come on, Jerry," Mrs. North said. "We can take them."

Mr. North looked at her, and his profile was disconsolate. He cross-courted in turn, off the forehand, and missed the side-line by inches— out. He banged his racket on the ground and himself on the forehead, with an open hand.

"Forty-fifteen," the umpire said, formally. "Match point," he added, out of sheer excitement. Mr. North glared at him.

Mrs. North won her point with a forehand down the alley.

"Forty-thirty," the umpire said, tensely.

Miss Corbin served with a sudden change of pace. Mr. North jumped in, barely caught it and everybody watched while it went off at an impossible angle, landed just over the net, and, under the impetus of an obviously unintended slice, bounced back into the Norths' court.

"Oh," said the girl beside Weigand. "Oh. Oh!" Everybody else said "Oh" except the umpire, who said "Deuce."

Miss Corbin rapped her racket angrily on the ground and said something to Mr. Saunders. Weigand didn't hear what it was, but it didn't sound pleasant. He saw Saunders flush a little under the sunburn.

"Keep your service deep, why don't you?" he said. "And come in!"

Miss Corbin served a fault and served again. Mrs. North let it go by, inches beyond the service line. Nobody said anything. The Norths looked at the linesman, who looked back blandly.

"Advantage Miss Corbin," the umpire said.

She served to Mr. North, who chopped back to her. She returned to Mrs. North, who drove for a tiny opening between her opponents, and found it. Miss Corbin and Mr. Saunders glared at each other. They were irritated, strained. It seemed to Weigand, watching them, that their irritation might have a background beyond the evident cause. But you couldn't tell. He watched Mr. North suddenly beam and go over to pat his wife on the shoulder. Miss Corbin served, set up another floater off Mrs. North's drive, and North killed it. Advantage out. She served again and Mr. North, suddenly revived, drove hard to her alley. Her backhand went into the net and she threw her racket down angrily. Then she picked it up and went ahead of her partner around the net as they changed courts. Her face was set and angry.

The Norths tied it at five-all on Mrs. North's service and then broke through Saunders—thanks in part to a missed volley by Miss Corbin, at which Saunders stared coldly. The Norths looked at their adversaries curiously and everybody sitting along the court seemed subdued and a little nervous. The final game was a rout, the Norths winning at love. There was a strange moment after the last point when a situation seemed to be stretching in the air; then Miss Corbin suddenly smiled and ran forward to the net to shake Mrs. North's hand. Then everybody shook hands and Miss Corbin and Saunders shook hands and it was only the end of a "bunny" tournament match.

The four came off court together and the Norths descended on Weigand joyfully.

"Bill!" Mrs. North said. "We won! Did you see? We won!"

Weigand looked down at her affectionately and said it was nice going. He shook hands with Mr. North, who said, "Hiya, Bill, was I *awful!*" Mrs. North said he must meet people and darted off toward her late opponents. A dark, active young man had an arm around Miss Corbin's shoulders and was saying, "You were going great, Jean." He spoke like a Southerner, Weigand thought. He congratulated Pam North when she came up, and a pale-haired young woman with a face which was suddenly bitter turned away from where she had been standing near Jean Corbin and the young Southerner. Then Jean Corbin, Saunders, the dark young man and Mrs. North turned back to North and Weigand, and came toward them. Mrs. North introduced.

"Jean," she said, "this is Bill Weigand. Jean Corbin. Hardie Saunders. John Blair. He's from Georgia. And—Bram, come here. Bram Van Horst. He owns us all." Bram Van Horst was a tall, very blond man in his middle forties, with hair receding from a domed head. He laughed at Pam's explanation of him, but did not amplify. Pam collected more.

It was a haze of people, too rapidly moving and confused even for Weigand's trained habits of identification. There was James Harlan Abel, who was Dr. Abel to Pam, and his wife, who was Evelyn. There was Thelma Smith—she was the pale-haired girl, who still looked bitter, but less bitter than she had. There was Helen Wilson, who was the girl who had given Weigand the score. There was a man named something Kennedy and a girl named Dorian something. Weigand's confusion lightened a little when Dorian entered it; she was a girl who moved with an arresting certainty of balance such as Weigand had seen only once or twice before—in a boxer, once, and again in a tennis player to whom, years before, Weigand had lost in the second round of a rather good tournament. The place was thick with people—a couple named Askew floated into and out of the group; a middle-aged man named Hanscomb arrived, inquired how Weigand did and vanished.

Then there was a tall, rangy man with a crooked smile and a familiar red head and beside him a slender, black-haired young woman in dark red slacks and a soft white shirt. She had a heart-shaped face and a diverting expression of impertinence.

"You know the Fullers," Pam North said. "Jane. Ben. Here's a friend of yours."

The Fullers looked at him, smiled, and looked at each other.

"Do we know him, kid?" Ben Fuller inquired. "Do we know guys like him?"

Jane Fuller thought, puckering her face.

"Maybe a little," she said. "Maybe we know him just a little."

They turned to Weigand.

"We think we know you a little," Fuller said. "How are you, fellow?"

"Fine," Weigand said. "On vacation, as it happens. If that's all right with you, Fuller?"

He grinned as he said it, and Fuller grinned back. They shook hands and Jane smiled at him. Then she whistled, lightly, a few bars from Gilbert and Sullivan. Weigand grinned at her, and said that just now there wasn't any to be done.

"Not for ten days, anyhow," he said. "Vacation. So don't start anything."

Then there were more people, drifting in, drifting away. Pam began what was evidently a move to corral.

"Drinks with us," she said. "Wait here."

Weigand, North and the Fullers waited in a small, expectant group while Mrs. North tapped guests. She tapped Helen Wilson and Helen brought the girl named Dorian, who still moved with that odd and challenging perfection of balance, to join the knot of the chosen. She tapped, in succession, Jean Corbin, who shook her head and smiled and said something, and Hardie Saunders, who nodded his head and smiled but did not join Mrs. North as she returned.

"Jean's going to Bram's," Mrs. North said. "And Hardie's got a stew, but he'll be along later."

She noticed a reeling expression on Weigand's face and smiled at him helpfully.

"A stew to put on," she said. "He and Johnny Blair share a cabin and Hardie cooks."

Weigand nodded, consoled. Mrs. North led them toward the cabin.

"Look," her husband said, apparently to the company at large. "I don't know about anybody else, but I'm going to take a shower."

"It's September!" Mrs. North said in a shocked tone. "I was thinking of a fire."

Mr. North said there could be a fire afterward, but it was warm, even if September, and he was showering.

"Anybody who wants—" he said. "You, Bill?"

Weigand was a little puzzled, but he said, "Right," because he supposed it would be. Mrs. North looked at them and shook her head.

"You always fix it," she said, "so that somebody else makes the drinks." She paused and looked at her assembly, moving idly up the slope to the cabin. "Ben can," she decided. "But we'll save you the fire."

And then the group scattered on the Norths' lawn and Pete met them and spoke urgently of the icebox, and the Norths moved Weigand and luggage into a room. It was a simple, rectangular cabin, with a spreading central living-room. There was a fireplace at one end and French doors opening on a terrace at the other. Three corner rooms were bedrooms, big enough for beds and chests of drawers; the fourth was the kitchen, big enough for stove and icebox and a clamoring cat, which was trying to get into the box.

"Liver," Mrs. North said. "He always does."

Weigand put on trunks as he was told and got a towel. Pete produced excited sounds indicating the arrival of liver; Ben Fuller moved toward the icebox and the liquor supply; Mr. North said "Tom Collinses, huh?" to Weigand and when Weigand nodded shouted "Two Toms" to Fuller. Then Weigand and North were going back the way they had come, past the tennis courts, and on along a path through reddening sumach, with the lake darting sunlight from the right.

"Well—" said Weigand.

"Isn't it?" North said. "But you'll get used to it. Do you mind cold showers?"

"Well—" said Weigand.

"Yes," North said. "I see what you mean. But it's swell afterward."

The path curved toward the lake through trees and came suddenly on a brook, crossed by a narrow bridge.

"Hello the shower?" Mr. North yelled, suddenly.

"Hello," said what was apparently the shower, in a feminine voice. "Just coming out."

They crossed the bridge and hesitated and after a moment Jean Corbin came out, in fresh white slacks and yellow shirt and with damp hair. She said "brrr!

"It's getting to be more than I can take," she said. "I freeze." She turned along another path away from them and called back, "See you at the Fullers'."

North led Weigand to the shower. It was a pipe extending from the top of the bank over the brook with a shower nozzle giving freely at the end.

"Right from a spring," Mr. North said, cheerfully, and climbed out of his trunks. Weigand watched him, and shivered. Mr. North went under and seemed to contract. "Wow!" said Mr. North. He soaped, gyrated, and emerged. "Feels swell," he said, chattering. Weigand wished himself elsewhere; or Mr. North elsewhere, taking any compulsion to manliness with him. But he braced himself and went under. When he could say anything he said "Jesus!" and it was more prayer than blasphemy. But it felt fine afterward.

They rubbed and resumed trunks and talked idly.

"A lot of people to meet at once, isn't it?" Mr. North said. Weigand nodded.

"They'll come to you as time goes on," North promised. "You'll be seeing them all after dinner, at the Fullers'. Party."

"Right," said Weigand.

Mr. North submerged himself in thought.

"Did you," he said suddenly, "ever see anything flukier than that shot of mine?"

Weigand said he hadn't, that he could remember.

• 2 •

SATURDAY
4 P.M. TO 6:30 P.M.

The people began to come straight a little as they sat in the cabin, before a tiny fire built, Mrs. North said, for cheerfulness. (But as the sun sank one began to remember that it was September; that they were sixty miles northeast of New York and five hundred feet higher.) Bram Van Horst came straight, for example. He owned Lone Lake and all the cabins. He had been an aviator once, and an army officer in the first world war and for a while he had been rather successful as an illustrator. Then he had bought a hundred and fifty acres and built a dam— "he's Dutch, you know," Mrs. North explained—and put up cabins around the edge of the lake when it filled. He called it Lone Lake—"I guess because he was lonely then," Mrs. North said—and rented the cabins to people he knew, or friends of people he knew.

Weigand sat, glass in hand, on a couch beside Dorian Hunt. The people were new to her, too. She hadn't, she said, been up before, although Helen had often asked her. Helen lived in what had been the farmhouse, when Lone Lake was a farm, commuting to New York in spite of unfriendly train schedules. Helen's mother stayed at the lake all summer, and took care of Helen and Helen's guests.

"She's a jolly soul," Dorian Hunt told Weigand, as this information weaved in and out of the conversation, broke off at some remark from Ben Fuller, started again when the talk hesitated and almost stilled. Weigand thought of the description the next day, when he met Mrs. Wilson, who then had no cause for jollity.

Dorian was a fashion artist and Arthur Kennedy, who was also a guest of the Wilsons', was a friend of hers and of Helen's.

"Misplaced at the moment, apparently," she added.

Weigand exchanged information, giving her the Fullers, Ben and Jane. They lived in the Village, in a house all their own, and Fuller was an importer like his father before him.

"I don't know them at all well, as a matter of fact," Weigand added. "I met them both once, in connection with a matter—well, a matter of business. Likable."

Dorian nodded, and looked off inquiringly at Helen Wilson, who was standing up, with a small package under her arm. Helen was a tall, solid girl with light hair and wholesome coloring. She told Dorian to stay right where she was.

"I've got to go to Ireland's," she said, "and then around to Jean's to leave her a tennis shirt I bought for her and forgot, and then I'll be back. Keep my drink warm for me." She looked around. "I'll put it up here," she said, and put it on the mantel. Then she went off along the path which paralleled the road toward Ireland's store. Everybody who had looked up and smiled returned to their drinks. Nobody could do more than guess afterward what time she left or returned, but she was gone, Weigand thought, not quite half an hour.

She came back, at any rate, took her drink, looked around at the others suspiciously, and said she had left more than that. "Lots more," she said. Everybody laughed and Mr. North made her a fresh one. He had only finished it, and one or two refills, including Weigand's, when somebody outside said: "Hello?"

The Norths said "Yo!" and Hardie Saunders came in, tall and blond and with a sunburn which seemed to glow in the room. He had a rum collins, and cupped his big hands around the tall glass gratefully. Then he looked at the little fire and snorted.

"My God," he said. "A fire!" He looked hot, and made much of it, mopping his forehead. "I thought fires were weeks off."

"Not in this house," Mrs. North said firmly. "Don't give Jerry ideas. He *never* gets cold and I have to build them and get kerosene all over me. Smelly."

"Kerosene?" Weigand said, looking at the logs blazing.

"To start," North said. "We all do up here. Old Marvin doesn't sell kindling, so we just slosh kerosene on and—pouff!"

"That's why we don't allow Boy Scouts," said Mrs. North. "They'd writhe so, the poor things."

The talk was now desultory, now heated as it turned to the world war that was beginning, shied away from it, edged relentlessly back. There were more drinks and Helen Wilson joined Dorian and Weigand on the couch. She seemed thoughtful, but listened smilingly when North and Saunders post-mortemed the mixed doubles final. Mr. North insisted gravely that he had all along intended the slice on his return of service.

"It was just as we planned it," he insisted. Saunders said, "Yah!" in burlesqued disgust. "Why, Jean and I—" he said. He left it at that and moved across the room away from the fire. He was out of earshot when Helen turned to Weigand.

"You can't imagine how odd that sounds," she said suddenly. "'Jean and I' from Hardie Saunders. As odd as that they should have been playing together—" She stopped and made a gesture of annoyance. "Although why they shouldn't," she said. "That I of all people should be starting gossip." She looked at Weigand and smiled. "Forget it," she said. "It was just that they used to be better friends than they are now and we were surprised when Jerry and Ben put them together, even if they do make a good team. But it worked out fine, didn't it? You saw them play together and particularly at first—but you didn't see them at first, did you?"

Weigand said he hadn't.

"They were playing so beautifully together," Helen said. "It was fun to watch them, even when they were losing the first set. And in the second—!"

There seemed to be nothing much to say.

"You know them well?" he asked.

Helen said she did. She and Jean Corbin worked in the same advertising agency, Bell, Halpern & Bell. And Saunders had been an account executive there until about a year before, when he had left to start his own agency, taking the account with him.

"Quench," Helen said. "Awful stuff. You drink it. Anyway, lots of people drink it."

"And what did Bell, Halpern & Bell think of that?" Weigand said.

They hadn't, naturally, been much pleased, but it was all in the game. Jean Corbin, who had been Saunders' assistant, became an account executive a month or two later, so it was all right with her. And Bell, Halpern & Bell weathered nicely.

"And all this," Helen said, "must bore you terribly. How did I get started?"

It wasn't clear to Weigand, who was watching Dorian Hunt's small, animated face as she talked to Ben Fuller, sitting in a chair pulled up in front of her.

"Is she—Miss Hunt—also with Bell and whatnot?" he said. Helen shook her head.

"Fashion artist," she said. "Free lance. And good; funny thin girls all her own."

People were, Weigand decided, coming to him as North had promised. For no good reason he checked them in his mind, recapitulating. Jane and Ben Fuller, whom he knew; Hardie Saunders, large and blond and sunburned, and proprietor of an advertising agency which advanced the claims of "Quench." Helen Wilson, hearty and wholesome and something—a copywriter, he would guess—with Bell, Halpern & Bell. Jean Corbin, account executive with the same, and slight, dark, with a face of clear pallor and features carved impeccably by an artist. Bram Van Horst, who had flown airplanes and commanded men and done illustrations, and now was the squire of Lone Lake, and was Dutch and built dams. And the Norths, whom he had met under such unprepossessing circumstances, and got to know under such stress and whom he had come to know much better during the year—the year less a month or so—since he had encountered them, and been puzzled by them. A year since Mrs. North, going upstairs to an empty apartment above hers in Greenwich Place, had found the bathroom so unexpectedly and horribly occupied.*

Then two things happened in quick succession. Fuller and Dorian Hunt were suddenly both looking at Weigand, Fuller grinning with the expression of light-hearted malice Weigand remembered from previous encounters. Dorian Hunt's expression was different—withdrawn, considering.

"I've been telling her about you, copper," Fuller said. "She was asking."

"Oh," said Weigand, flatly because Dorian Hunt's face made him feel flat. "Right."

Then there was a peculiar cat sound at the door and Pete shouldered open the screen. He was staggering under the weight of a quarter-grown rabbit, clamped in his jaws. Over the rabbit, Pete's eyes shone with pride. All the women gave small squeals of horror, but Dorian Hunt moved.

She was across the room in an instant and had the surprised cat by the neck. With a kind of desperateness in her movements, she wrested the rabbit from Pete, who yowled in disapproval but was too polite to scratch. The rabbit was wide-eyed with terror, but still alive.

"You—!" Dorian Hunt stormed at Pete. "You—hunter!"

Pete, not used to humans who were other than friendly, backed away, one yellow eye wistfully on the rabbit which Dorian held to her, while little drops of blood dripped unnoticed on her bare arm. Then Dorian looked abashed and apologetic, and spoke more gently to Pete. She told Pete that it was his way, and that he was a cat and knew no better.

"If only they wouldn't hunt!" she said, turning to the others. "They're so gracious and beautiful, but they hunt." She stroked the rabbit. "It's trembling," she said. "It's dreadful to be hunted."

Nobody said anything, because there seemed to be nothing to say.

* The circumstances of Mrs. North's discovery are described in "The Norths Meet Murder." .

Then Mrs. North, deftly, broke the moment and turned it against Pete. She told Pete he was a bad cat, a dreadful cat, and pushed him out the door. He went, looking back at the rabbit. Mr. North took the rabbit from Dorian and said he would see it safe and was gone a little while and came back without rabbit and with reassurance. They brought Pete in, then, and shut the door so he would forget and he went to rub against Dorian's bare legs, forgivingly. After a moment, she stroked him and repeated, to him and the company at large, that of course he didn't know any better.

But she did not, from then until the time she and Helen, and the Fullers and Saunders with them, left the Norths' cabin, look directly at Lieutenant William Weigand, acting captain in the Homicide Bureau of the New York Police Department. It was pretty clear, Weigand thought—and was depressed unexpectedly by the thought—that she didn't like detectives. She felt more strongly about them, he suspected, than a charming young woman in her middle twenties ought to have any reason to feel.

• 3 •

SATURDAY
6:30 P.M. TO SUNDAY, 1:25 A.M.

Lieutenant Weigand believed that a detective needed luck, and that a lucky detective was given hunches. He thought, afterward, that a particularly lucky detective would have had a hunch during the Fullers' party; would have felt in the air something of what was coming, as the thunder of a summer storm announces what is to come, making ash-trays tremble metallically and sending vibrations tingling through glass. But Weigand was not that lucky, and no hunch troubled him all the evening. And since no hunch told him that he should, he paid no more than any man's attention to what went on.

It was a casual party. The Norths led him to it along a path through the sumach, reddening for autumn, a little after nine, and already it was dark. They had had another drink after the rest left, and a steak and an hour or so of sitting while the setting sun did things to clouds which made Mrs. North say "Oh," and then while it grew dark, with the air of having all the time in the world to grow dark. They talked lazily, and the Norths gossiped a little. What Helen Wilson had meant about Jean Corbin and Hardie Saunders was that they had once been, everybody believed, in love, but that it had broken off after Saunders left the advertising agency.

16

"Jean gets around," Mrs. North said, with tolerance. "Now it's Johnny Blair, from 'way down south in Dixie. Which made Thelma very annoyed."

Weigand tried to remember.

"Thelma?" he said. "Which one was Thelma?"

"Pale," Mrs. North said. "No-colored, stringy hair. She was at the court. Sort of forgettable face and always looks unhappy, sort of."

"Oh, yes," Weigand said. "What annoyed her?"

"She thought she was going to be Cinderella again," Mrs. North said. "You'd be sorry if she'd let you like her. But there wasn't any prince."

Weigand looked at Mr. North, who shook his head and said he'd tell it, since it had been brought up.

"Thelma shared a cabin with Jean last year," he said. "And the year before. They used to be great friends, although I always thought Jean had Thelma around—well, for whatever reason it is that attractive women sometimes like to have unattractive ones around." He held up a restraining hand toward Mrs. North, who seemed inclined to yip. "I said *sometimes*," he said. "Not you, wiggles."

"And don't call me '*wiggles*'!" Mrs. North said.

Mr. North captured the hand which was beating his arm, and continued.

"Then, toward the end of last season, Blair turned up and was over at the Jean-Thelma cabin a good deal. He lives with Saunders, and Saunders introduced him. And Thelma seems to have been a little confused for a while as to his purposes. Then Jean and Blair, between them, unconfused her. And Jean and Thelma stopped sharing a cabin. Clear?"

"Well—" said Weigand, speculatively. "She's still here, though. Thelma, I mean."

"She's just up for the party tonight," North said. "She's staying overnight at the Wilsons', or somewhere. Jane Fuller thought it would be nice to invite her."

"But you're not telling him about James Harlan Abel," Mrs. North objected. "Our only professor. And Jean after him."

"Look," North said, "I don't see how we got into this. Does Bill *have* to know about all these people?"

"Yes," said Mrs. North. "It's fascinating. Like a comedy or something."

"Well," North said, and hesitated. "We think that now Jean is getting a little fed up with Johnny Blair and would like to go over to Abel. Abel's tall, stooped, and young-looking in an old way—you met him. He's at Columbia. English. He's new this year, and Jean apparently likes him. Or just likes his being new. Anyway, the sewing circle is mighty suspicious about it, and is very sorry for Mrs. Abel, who is old-looking in a young sort of way. She's the one with faintly red hair. Very thin and nervous. She rides herd on James Harlan, rather, and our Jeanie had better look out."

Mr. North paused a moment.

"And now," he said, "shall we tell you how Van Horst beats his wife?"

"Jerry!" said Mrs. North, indignantly. "You're making fun!"

Mr. North was very grave.

"We think you should know all," he assured Weigand. "This is a very desperate place, full of currents. We're just waiting until Van Horst gets married."

Mrs. North got her hand loose and resumed pounding her husband's arm, with an indignation which was not supposed to convince.

That had all been just before they went along the path through the sumach to the party at the Fullers'. The Fuller cabin was very like the Norths', only rather larger, as it shortly needed to be. It was a casual but crowded party; Weigand met all the people he had met before or heard talked about, and a good many others and after a few drinks he found a place to sit in a corner and the party became a pleasant blur. He hoped Dorian Hunt would sit by him when there was a place vacant, but she didn't. A few times he danced with Pam North and Jane Fuller, when there was dancing, and Saunders sat beside him for a few minutes, looking damply hot and jovial, and Helen Wilson said that she didn't want to dance, but that a drink and a place to sit would save her life. So for a time after he had got her a fresh drink she sat beside Weigand, companionably but without saying much.

People went in and out of the cabin on excursions and for purposes of their own. Weigand went out once and found that white mist was rising from the lake and that an almost full moon had come up and was shining on it and as he turned back into the house he met Hardie Saunders coming out, mopping his forehead and talking about air. Helen Wilson was gone from her place on the sofa when he got back, but after a little he saw her dancing. Both the Norths were gone, then, and so was Jean Corbin, who had been talking quickly, containedly, to a thin, oldish-young man who must be James Harlan Abel. But Mrs. Abel seemed nowhere in sight to ride herd. Then the Norths came back, apparently having been somewhere in a car, the lights of which swept the lawn outside the cabin and went out just before they came in. Van Horst was with them and with Van Horst was a guitar, and then he sang Scottish and Irish songs, and one or two songs of surprising bawdiness.

It was then and afterward that a hunch would have been helpful, but Weigand had no hunch. So he paid only the attention that a man comfortably looking on at a party, a reasonable part of the time through the bottom of a glass, might be expected to pay. He had, when he tried to work things out afterward, a belief that most of the people he knew at the party had been grouped around, on chairs and sofas and the floor, when Van Horst was singing. But he had no definite guess to make as to what time that was. And as, afterward, the party scattered from the nucleus of the music, and took on a more rapid tempo, he made no effort to follow the movements of the various Lone Lakers. Dorian Hunt was, he was pretty sure, out of the cabin only once or twice, and then briefly, and he was surprised, when it came time to remember what he could, how sharply he remembered her—now dancing with the grace he had expected; now standing and talking, and managing to carry that rather singular, balanced grace even into relative immobility. Her smile recognized him once or twice, but when he tried to get her to dance she had already moved into the arms of someone else.

It was, he knew, very near the end of the party when Jean Corbin ended a dance near where he was sitting, and sat down beside him and said:

"They say you are a detective."

Weigand nodded.

"I'm trying," he said, "to be on vacation, though." He patted his pockets. "No handcuffs," he added. "No gun." The gun was back at the Norths', locked in a bag, and he had no handcuffs. There was a badge in his pocket, however.

"It must be interesting," Jean Corbin said. "Thinking ahead of people. Outwitting them. Letting them think they are too clever and then—snap!"

Weigand smiled and said it seldom worked out that way. Usually, he said, it was a question of getting hold of somebody who knew something, and getting him to tell what he knew. A stool-pigeon; a man who might be expected to grow talkative if he had to go too long without narcotics; a man who stayed unmolested on sufferance, and the promise of a willing tongue. Those things, and what one came to know of certain patterns of criminal behavior.

"I don't mean professional criminals," the slim, dark girl with the sharply cut face assured him. "I mean—oh, murderers who haven't police records or anything, and kill—what shall I say?—privately, for private ends."

Weigand nodded, and said he assumed she did. Most people thought of crime like that, he said. But most crime was professional and its detection took a memory for faces and for facts, and a knowledge of who, among all the talkers the department knew of, might be the man to talk to the point. That and organization, and having plenty of men to cover the ground.

"It's seldom the detective's wits against those of the gentlemanly murderer," he said. "Too bad, isn't it?"

"But sometimes—?" she insisted.

Weigand said of course, sometimes. And that then it was usually a lot of work, with no assurance of success.

"Murder is seldom ingenious, outside books," he said. "And when it is, it is often successfully hidden." He grinned at her. "Only don't try it," he added. "Sometimes we *do* catch on, and you might be unlucky."

She shook her head and said she wouldn't.

"Not even Hardie, the lummox," she said. "Although when he let that one get by this afternoon I could have—"

Saunders' ears apparently caught their owner's name, to which ears are always so marvelously attuned. At any rate, he came over and stood in front, and beamed down.

"What's this I hear?" he demanded. "What's this?"

"I was telling him I thought I was going to have to kill you because of this afternoon," Jean explained. "But he talked me out of it. You owe him your life."

"Good," Saunders said. "Thanks, old man. Keep an eye on her, will you? They say you're a cop."

He seemed pleasantly drunk and amiable.

Jean looked at the watch on her wrist, and said suddenly that she thought she would go. It was after one, she said, impossible as it sounded. The party seemed unabated but, as Weigand looked it over, it was appreciably thinned out. Dorian had gone, for one, and apparently Helen Wilson with her; the discontented face of Thelma Smith also had vanished. The Abels, together now, and the Norths, also together, were talking and Mrs. North caught Weigand's eye and her eyebrows indicated Jean and went up. Both Fullers were mixing drinks and somebody was urging Van Horst to play again. Jean got up and drew a light coat around her.

"Is your cabin near?" Weigand asked. "Should I walk along with you?"

She smiled and said it would be nice, if he wanted to. They walked through a mist that was creeping higher from the lake and now dulled Weigand's flashlight as they went along a path which seemed to circle the lake. The path dipped toward the lake, and another joined it from the right and the sumach was still growing closely. Then Jean turned up, away from the water, and the moonlight outlined another cabin, rather smaller than the others. They stepped in and Jean said to wait a moment while she got a light. A match flared and she lighted lamps. Then she said "brrr!

"It's cold in here," she said. "The fire's—well, that's odd. It isn't quite out, is it? It's smoldered along since this morning, evidently."

Bill Weigand crossed to the fireplace.

"It needs stirring," he said, and stirred it resolutely. A flame shot up.

"It needs more wood," Weigand said. "If you'll tell me where—?"

"In the still-room," she said. "Through that door."

The Corbin cabin differed from the others Weigand had seen. It was considerably smaller, in its central mass. But a one-room wing had been built beyond the kitchen; built solidly, with a concrete floor. There was wood piled in it, and a few garden tools and a two-gallon can for kerosene. Weigand picked up an armful of wood, went back, built up the fire and said:

"Still-room?"

Jean was sitting on a bench in front of the fire, huddling toward it. She held out her hands to the flame as she explained.

"It *was* a still-room," she said. "Really a still-room. That was before I took the cabin. The man who had had it was a broker before 1929, and then he turned bootlegger in a small way, and Van Horst let him build a room. He made it solider than the rest of the cabin, I guess to keep the fumes in, or something. So I store things in it—wood and kerosene and just general rubbish."

Her voice sounded tired, Weigand decided. And, anyway, the Norths would wonder about him. She thanked him for building up the fire, and for being company, but did not urge that he stay. The mist had grown thicker when Weigand stepped out into it, and took a path which he thought was the one they had come by. And almost instantly he was lost, because this path branched and dwindled and seemed to cross another, and ended at a long, rough dock extending into the lake. A boat floated at the end of the dock.

The mist which baffled the flashlight, and the crossing paths and the close-growing sumach, proved unexpectedly difficult. Weigand tried one path, but it ended in a dark cabin which was not the Corbin cabin. Another ended in an outhouse. A third seemed to abandon life entirely in the thick of the undergrowth. Weigand said, "Damn!" when he came to that. He began to feel that he had been pushing his way through the mist for a long time. Then for the first time in hours, he turned his flashlight beam on his wristwatch. It showed 1:20. He must, he thought, already have been gone from the Corbin cabin almost a quarter of an hour, and he had evidently got no place. He stopped and listened.

"Oh, oh, my honey, have a—on me!" he heard. That was the party. He could fill in the pause, because he had heard it filled in before. Everybody was singing, and when they came to the pause they all sniffed resolutely. "Morphine Bill and Cocaine Sue" was being shouted happily to his right. He turned toward it, and found the faintest of the paths. He started along it and then, drawing in his breath quickly, he stopped.

There was something dark and inert lying across the path in front of him, and when his light found it, it was the body of a woman. She lay face down, sprawled shapelessly, and around her head dark wetness caught the light from his torch. Weigand had seen enough death to know he was seeing it again. He bent quickly to throw the light on the face, and to see it he had to lift the head a little. He was flooded, as he did so, with the certainty that he already knew what he would see. And then he let his breath out so that the tiny rush of it was almost a whistle.

Because what he saw was not what he had, in that moment, known he would see. What he saw was the face of Helen Wilson.

Helen Wilson was dead. In the left side of her throat was a ragged gash. But blood was not flowing from it any longer.

• 4 •

Weigand was a man on vacation in the country when he knelt beside the body, but he was a policeman when he stood up. He was a cop and wanted more cops. He moved away from the body, remembering where he stepped, and around it in a wide circle, bending under the low, branching crowns of the sumach. When he came out on a path it was only a little distance from the Fullers' cabin, and he covered the distance quickly. But at the door he paused a moment and then entered casually. It would have been hard to detect more than casual greeting in Weigand's glance when it caught Mr. North's eyes. Mr. North, looking a little surprised, came across to him.

Weigand's hand, pressing on his friend's arm, guided him out of the cabin and to a shadow.

"Something—?" Mr. North said. Weigand nodded.

"Yes," he said. "The Wilson girl. Down in the sumach."

His tone told more than his words.

"Somebody—?" North began, and then there was a quick movement beside them.

24

"Something's happened!" Mrs. North said. "Jerry—are you all right, Jerry? Bill?"

You didn't keep things from Mrs. North, or try to. Weigand, speaking quickly, without emphasis, told them what he had found.

"No!" Mrs. North said. "No. Not *again*."

Weigand nodded.

"More than your share," he agreed. "One murder ought to have been enough, certainly." He paused. "More than hers, too," he said. "There's something wrong about it. She wasn't the one asking for it."

"No," said Mrs. North. "Oh, it's dreadful. She was— She was so nice. And our lovely lake!" She paused. "Our *lake*," she said. She was silent, her hand on her husband's arm, convulsively tight. They waited for her a moment and then she said: "All right, now. What do we do?"

She, Weigand told her, did nothing—or rather, she went back to the party and showed nothing, which would be a lot to do. North went to a telephone—"Ireland's?" Weigand asked, and North nodded. They needed State policemen, fast. He would be waiting where the body was.

"I don't want anybody—cleaning up," he said.

The Norths nodded. Mrs. North breathed deeply, so that she was no longer trembling, and Mr. North moved off along a path, casually at first and then more quickly. Weigand lighted a cigarette, looked around, and was gone in the mist.

It was hardest for Mrs. North. It was hard to take up a drink again; hard to listen to Dr. Abel, who was talking about the war, and the turning times which made might seem right again, and speculating whether the human animal could, after all, find another basis which would not crumble. "The right to act as you please, taking responsibility for the act," he said. "Accepting another's right, the group's right, to stop you, to retaliate. Perhaps those are the only rights—to protect yourself." It sounded vague, academic, almost meaningless, when you were waiting for the cry of sirens.

And then there was no cry of sirens. After a few long minutes Jerry North came back, and smiled at someone and lifted a drink from a tray and came across to her, still smiling. His fingers touched her arm and there was pressure for a moment, and assurance, and when she looked at him his eyes seemed to nod an answer to her question, although his head did not move. It was almost no time after that before there was the bumping purr of a motorcycle engine, and with it Mr. North drew her away, and out of the cabin into the shadow which the house blacked out of the moonlight.

A State trooper was propping up his motorcycle and then coming toward them. The moonlight shone on him and then he was in the shadow.

"North?" he said. "Gerald North? You're the man who telephoned?"

"Down here," North said. "You'll want to talk to Weigand."

"Yes?" said the trooper. "All right."

Weigand heard them coming. His flashlight glowed a moment in the mist, then went out; then glowed again. Weigand said, "Hello, trooper," in a cop's voice and the trooper looked at him curiously. Then the trooper looked down and said:

"Christ!"

"Yes," Weigand said. "That's the way it is, trooper. You'll want to get on the phone."

The trooper knelt by the body.

"Yeh," he said. "Only I did, mister. The B.C.I. boys will be along."

He stood up.

"Who are you, lady?" he said to Mrs. North. "Who brought you here? And you, fellow—who are you?"

Weigand told him and he said, "Oh, yeah?" Weigand's hand came out of his pocket with a badge cupped in the palm. "Yes, sir," the trooper said. "Lieutenant Heimrich will be along. You want to tell me anything, Lieutenant?"

Weigand said he could tell what he knew, and did. He said that, except the Norths, nobody else knew.

"One other guy knows," the trooper said.

"Yes," Weigand said. "One other guy knows, all right. But we'll wait for Heimrich. He's coming from Hawthorne?"

The trooper said he was, with some of the boys. And perhaps somebody from the D.A.'s office, and the medical examiner. "They'll come from Carmel, though," he explained. "They ought to be here first."

Weigand nodded.

"What do we do?" Mr. North asked. "We just wait? Who do we wait for?"

"Men from the B.C.I.—Bureau of Criminal Identification—of the State Police," Weigand told him. "They called it a 'Scotland Yard' in the papers for a while. It's a specially trained detective force, with detachments in each of the main barracks—each with an inspector, ranked as a lieutenant, in charge. They take over for the district attorneys in counties, like this, where they don't run to county detectives." He paused, looking down at the body. "They're pretty good, too, aren't they, trooper?"

"Yes, sir," the trooper said. "They're pretty good."

They came after a little, and this time there were sirens and then there was no keeping it from anybody. Lieutenant Heimrich was a short, powerful man in civilian clothes, and there were a sergeant and two troopers with him, also out of uniform. And there were other troopers on motorcycles and more in two open cars. Still later, although they had a much shorter distance to come, there was a little, fussy man who owned a large, resonant voice and the title of district attorney, and a physician from the medical examiner's office. But by that time the Fullers' party had shattered, and photographers' lights tore through the fog to center on and around Helen Wilson's body, and there were men tramping through the sumach and calling heavily to one another. The Norths were back in the Fuller cabin, then, and troopers sat with what remained of the party.

Van Horst stood with Weigand and Heimrich near the body while the doctor bent over it, and held a flashlight close to the wound and shook his head. Then, after a good while, there was the clang of an ambulance bell on the road and new lights swept the Fullers' lawn, cluttered with cars and motorcycles, and two men carried a long bundle off on a stretcher.

And after that Heimrich appeared in the door of the Fuller cabin and looked over those who were still there, and Weigand came in behind him and looked, too, and smiled faintly at Jerry and Pam North, and at the Fullers when his eyes met theirs.

"All right," Heimrich said, suddenly, gratingly. "You can all go home and to bed. All of you who live here at the lake, or are visiting here. Are there any who don't?"

Nobody answered.

"O.K.," Heimrich said. "Go to your cabins and stick around. Don't try to go anywhere. Stay inside."

Weigand's lips twisted a little and he said something, softly, to the State Police lieutenant.

"Yeh," Heimrich said. "Sure." He looked at the very sobered civilians. "Only don't go any farther than your cabins, get me?" he said. Nobody said anything for a moment, and then Mrs. North said, unexpectedly:

"Thank you."

Heimrich looked at her darkly and then almost smiled. It was a very transient smile, however.

"Very well," he said. "Get along. I'll have men scattered around, so if anybody had thought of leaving—" He paused. "As I figure it," he said, "only one of you would want to leave. If I were in his place, I wouldn't try it."

He turned, suddenly, said "See you in the morning?" to Weigand, and went out. Weigand's eyes beckoned the Norths. The three of them went back along the path to the Norths' cabin, where the fire still burned. Mr. North piled logs on it.

"Well," he said, "what did they find out?"

"Not much," Weigand said. "Yet," he added. "They will, though—they're good at the job." He hesitated. "Don't spread anything I tell you, of course," he said. "Here's what we—they—know so far."

Helen Wilson had been dead for some time when Weigand stumbled on her body. She had been stabbed in the throat, with, apparently, a bulky and dull knife, which had torn as well as cut. She had been standing, probably facing her murderer, and had been struck a few feet from where she fell. Blood had spurted out on the sumach. She had twisted in falling, away from the murderer. The murderer had, apparently, then forced his way through the sumach toward the lake, although that was not certain.

"There was a broken branch," Weigand said. "We'll look for blood in the morning—the knife may have dripped."

"Ou—!" said Mrs. North. "How horrible. With the moonlight on it—"

"He may have been going to throw the weapon in the lake," Weigand said. "Or he may have wanted—well, to wash."

Mr. North nodded.

"The blood would have spurted, I suppose?" he said. "So he probably couldn't have come back to the party. It would have been on his clothes. If it was, of course, somebody from the party."

Weigand said it looked that way. That was one reason why Heimrich had not held those still at the party for immediate questioning. That, and the desire to know as much as he could before he started questioning.

"He wants light on it," Weigand said. "Literally as well as figuratively. The fog makes it worse. His idea is to keep everybody rounded up until morning, when he can see how people look by something better than kerosene lamps. He figures that any cleaning up the murderer had to do has already been done, so there'll be no harm."

"And you—?" Mr. North said.

Weigand said he was merely a bystander, like anyone else. Possibly he would have asked a question or two at once, but Heimrich's way was—well, Heimrich's way.

"He's a good man," Weigand said. "I've heard of him. Thorough, steady. He figures he can thrash it out in the morning when there's less excitement, and when he knows more."

"But if something else happens before he gets started—" Mrs. North said. "If the murderer *didn't* have everything cleaned up?" She paused. "Do you feel there's something funny about it?" she asked the two men, suddenly. They looked at her, and saw that her eyes were wide and rather frightened.

"Well—" said Mr. North and then he stopped and looked at Weigand. Weigand looked at them both a moment and then he nodded.

"Yes," he said. "It feels funny. You know why, don't you?"

"Say it," North said. "Go on, say it."

Weigand stood a moment, apparently thinking. Then he spoke softly.

"Only that it's the wrong girl," he said. "But I told Heimrich and he thinks I'm crazy. He says she was facing the murderer and she couldn't have been the wrong one. The murderer would have known."

"But it was dark," Mrs. North insisted.

Weigand said that was precisely the point. It wasn't dark; not there and then, and as she was standing when she began to die.

"You see," he said, "the moonlight was full on her face. It couldn't have been a mistake."

• 5 •

SUNDAY
8:15 A.M. TO 11 A.M.

There was the sound of a coarse file rasped on the edge of an opened tin can and Weigand sat up in bed, angrily. The crow left a limb of the aging apple tree outside Weigand's window and went to sit on a rock with another crow. Both of them dragged coarse files across the edges of opened tin cans. Weigand looked at his watch and learned that it was fifteen minutes past eight. He went to the window and stared at the crows and made bitter remarks about the peace of sleep in the country; about the peace of anything in the country.

"Murders and crows!" Weigand told himself, indignantly, and pulled on sneakers over heavy woolen socks, gray slacks and a faded blue sweater. Then the scream froze him as he reached for a hairbrush. It was a woman's scream and the sunlight shattered to let it through. It was a scream of terror and agony and for a moment it seemed to be everywhere. Then Weigand realized that it came diagonally across the lake from the north. He was out of his room and across the living-room, running, and on the porch. The scream came again, higher for a moment and then decrescendo with a horrible bubble in it. Then it was cut off.

"My God!" said North, suddenly beside Weigand. "What—?"

They stared down the lake, fixed. Smoke puffed up behind trees where the lake curved at the north and as they watched flame shot through it. Then a man shouted hoarsely from somewhere in that direction and there was the snort of a started motor. A siren whirred suddenly and there were more shouts. Weigand and North were over the porch rail, running toward the smoke. Mrs. North, in a rust-red robe, was on the porch behind them and the moment of time swelled up like a balloon. Then a man in State Police uniform came running around the cabin and went heavily, still running, down the path after her husband and Weigand. The moment broke and the porch door slammed behind Mrs. North as she ran back across the living-room.

The clock on the chest said 8:21 as Mrs. North threw off the robe, jabbed herself into shorts and fumbled with buttons. She pulled on an old-rose sweater, fuzzy and high at the throat, and laced sneakers over her bare feet. Then she was running, too, down the path toward the rising smoke, through which flames laced. Men were shouting and there was the feel of someone running behind her and then, over the hills, there was the despairing cry of a siren and under it the distant roar of a heavy motor, running fast.

It wasn't the Fullers'. She knew that even before she saw their cabin dark in the shadow of an elm. Jane Fuller, in a blue overall, stood on the shadowed porch and cried, "Jean's!" when Mrs. North ran toward her. She ran down the porch steps as Mrs. North paused and another trooper ran past her, brushing against the sleeve of the rose sweater. Jane ran on ahead of Mrs. North down the path which dipped toward the lake.

Flame was leaping through the roof of Jean Corbin's cabin and the heat forced them back. But already the fire truck from Patterson was crunching backward through the sumach and men were piling off it. Four ran with the end of a heavy hose toward the lake and two more spun the hose off the reel behind them. There were troopers and men from the cabins standing, held back by the heat. North and Weigand were well up, shielding their faces with their arms. Then the motor of the fire truck pounded and the hose swelled as water came through it from the lake. The nozzle dribbled, the stream arched from it, stiffened. There was a roar and a cloud of steam as it struck the fire.

The flames were less all-conquering than they had looked to be. They fought the water, angrily, and subsided under it. Smoke and steam swirled up, died down.

"Got it!" one of the firemen shouted.

"Hold it off from the door," Lieutenant Heimrich ordered. "We're going in."

He and a trooper ran forward and North and Weigand ran with them. They were gone inside as Mrs. North cried:

"No! Don't!" after them.

Then they were out again, dragging something and the water swished back where they had been, pouring through the door, drowning a red glow which licked at their heels. The four men were blackened, but the thing they drew after them out of the fire was blacker still and motionless. And horrible.

There was nothing to do for Jean Corbin. There had not been anything to do for her since that scream of agony bubbled at the end and stopped half finished. There would have been nothing to do for her even then.

Mr. North left the group and came to his wife and Jane Fuller, who were standing close together, and pulled both of them against him and then back from the group which had gathered around the charred body.

"There's nothing to do," he said. "Come away. There's nothing—"

"Jean?" Pam North said, in a voice with not enough breath behind it.

Mr. North nodded, then hesitated and nodded again.

"Yes," he said. "It would have to be, though it's hard to tell anything from—"

Then Weigand detached himself from the group and came toward them, and as he came he nodded to the question in North's eyes.

"Yes," he said. "Yes, it's Jean Corbin."

"She—" said Mrs. North. "It was a dreadful way, wasn't it?"

Weigand nodded.

"Only it wasn't long," he said. "That's all you can say. She was in the center of it, and it was all over her—in—well, I should think in a kind of puff."

Then Heimrich called him and he went back to the group and the two talked together for a moment, and Weigand nodded. Then, while the firemen from Patterson still poured water on the cabin, troopers went to the little groups in which the Lone Lakers had gathered and said a few words and the groups broke and melted.

"Go back to your cabins, the lieutenant says," a trooper told the Norths and Jane Fuller, and Ben Fuller, as, leaving one of the other groups, he came to them. "Go to your own cabins and stay in them until he gets to you, the lieutenant says."

They started off.

"Hey, North!" Weigand called, and Mr. North turned back. When Mrs. North went along the path and looked back he was standing with Heimrich and Weigand and a sergeant and one of the firemen, and they were looking at the cabin, which was only smoking a little, now. Almost half the cabin, and the still-room wing, seemed hardly to have been touched by the fire, Mrs. North noticed.

She went into the Fullers' cabin and they looked at one another and Fuller said, "Christ," in a strange, flat tone. Then Jane made coffee and they drank it and said very little. After a rather long time Mr. North looked in and said, "Come on up to the cabin, Pam." The Norths went together along the path and Mr. North held his wife's arm and then, after a moment, her hand. Neither of them said anything.

Weigand and Heimrich were at the cabin and as the Norths went in Weigand was talking.

"I don't see what other way it could be," he said. "But these people live here; they know how people do things here. We'll put it up to them."

Heimrich looked at the other policeman with doubt and inquiry in his expression. Weigand smiled suddenly, briefly, and said he would guarantee it.

"Wash them out," he said. "I had to, once. I'll guarantee it."

"Well—" Heimrich said. "So—"

"Here's the setup," Weigand said to the Norths. "We want your guess on it."

They had, he said, examined the cabin. The fire had apparently started near the fireplace, swept up the wall and through the roof. Jean Corbin's body had been near the door, fallen toward it. The door was in the same wall as the fireplace and she had been cut off by the flames.

"Not," Weigand said, "that that would have made any difference, apparently. She must have been in front of the fire when it—leaped at her."

Mr. North raised inquiring eyebrows.

"Right," Weigand said. "Wait."

The fire had burned more rapidly than it was easy to explain; more rapidly and fiercely, but over a comparatively limited area, with the fireplace as the center. The fireplace had several logs in it, only partly burned. The bench in front of the fireplace was almost burned through when they got in. A closed door had kept the flames out of the still-room wing, and out of the kitchen, and nothing in either room was touched.

"Now," Weigand said, "I was there about one-fifteen and built up the fire so that it would last the night. The fire was burning when I got there, but it was almost done and—" He paused suddenly. "Here's something I forgot," he said. "She was surprised that it was still burning; said she had started it in the morning but left it to die out during the day. She said something about its being better wood than she had thought. That may hook in."

"But how—?" Mrs. North said. "You think her nightgown or something—a robe, maybe—swished into the fire when she was starting it up and then—?"

Weigand said that it could, of course, have been that way. He looked at Heimrich.

"It still could have been," Heimrich said. "So—We don't know it wasn't. We're guessing."

"You people start fires with kerosene, don't you?" Weigand asked the Norths, while he held up a hand toward Heimrich. "You and most of the people here, because it's quicker and Marvin doesn't sell kindling?"

North nodded and said yes.

"But," he said, "kerosene—I mean, we've all used it for years. It was—a camp custom, you might call it."

"Everybody used it?" Weigand insisted. "It would be a safe guess by anybody that any other person up here used a cup or two of kerosene, poured over the logs, when he wanted to start a fire?"

"Sure," said Mr. North, while Mrs. North nodded. "But listen. Everybody here knows how to handle it—how much to put on, to stand back and toss a match if it is hot and smokes up and—"

Weigand held up a hand at him.

"Right," he said. "Now—"

They had checked over the cabin and, in the still-room, found a full two-gallon kerosene can. "Or almost full," Weigand added. There was a little spilled around it, as if it had only recently been picked up, or set down, hurriedly so that some of the liquid came out of the spout. It had hardly got warm in the still-room, so there hadn't been a fire. And—

"I touched the can," Weigand said. "Then I accidentally, more or less, smelled my hand, and it smelled funny for kerosene. Then we investigated."

"And it was—?" North said.

Weigand nodded.

"Yes," he said. "It wasn't kerosene in the can. It was gasoline."

Mr. North drew in his breath, sharply, but Mrs. North looked puzzled.

"You mean she was starting fires with gasoline?" she said. "But wouldn't that be an awful risk? And wouldn't she know if she made a hab—" Then Mrs. North drew in a breath.

"But she didn't," Mrs. North said, quickly. "I know she didn't, because just last week we were there for drinks in the evening and she was chilly—she got chilly awfully easy—and she built a fire and she said something about kerosene being the fire-maker's friend and—"

She looked at the men, wide-eyed.

"Right," Weigand said, and Heimrich said, slowly, "So—"

"But you couldn't use gasoline," Mrs. North said. "Gasoline explodes." She thought a moment. "But this didn't explode," she said. "The can was full, and if she poured it on the fire the fire would run up the stream and the can would blow up and—"

She stopped, because Weigand was shaking his head at her, and then looking at Heimrich with some hidden meaning in his glance.

"Exactly!" Weigand said. "That's what people think." He looked at Heimrich. "Just as I argued," he said. Then he turned back to Mrs. North and explained. She was wrong about the way gasoline acted; most people were. Most people thought of it as an explosive, like dynamite. But it wasn't. Most people thought that if you poured from a can onto a fire, or even onto embers, the stream from the can would ignite, fire would run up it and the can would explode.

"But all that gasoline commonly does," he said, "is to burn rapidly. You can get it to explode only under certain circumstances—roughly, when it is mixed with air in an inclosed space. Kerosene will explode under those conditions, too, but not so easily. If you want to and are careful, you can start fires with gasoline in reasonable safety. You can—and men on construction work frequently do—start fires with dynamite.

"Not that I'd recommend it," he added.

But you couldn't use gasoline in starting fires, or for any other purpose, precisely as you would use kerosene. "That's the point just now," Weigand said. You would have to take special precautions. You would have to be unusually careful.

"But Jean always was," Mrs. North said. "She poured kerosene on the logs and then carried the can back into the still-room where she kept it and shut the door—she always shut the door, but she carried the can away so it wouldn't be near the fire."

Weigand nodded, slowly. He seemed satisfied, as if something had been reaffirmed. He said, "Right," and then, after a moment, that that was the way he had figured it.

"What would *you* do?" he asked the Norths. "If you were Jean building a fire—how would you go about it?"

"Well," North said, "I pile in some logs, smaller ones at the bottom. Then I pour on some kerosene. If there's a fire there at all—or embers—it catches of itself in a minute or two with a kind of puff and spreads over the logs, which catch. That is, they usually catch. If there isn't a fire, sometimes the kerosene sort of smokes and then I stand back and toss a match in the smoke and it puffs. That's if the fireplace is still hot, I guess. If the fireplace is cold, I just hold a match to the kerosene and it catches, slowly."

Weigand said, "Right.

"Now," he said, "do you know what would happen if, instead of kerosene, you poured gasoline—about as much gasoline as you'd use kerosene; say you didn't know the difference—on embers and—"

"Smell," said Mrs. North. Everybody looked at her inquiringly.

"They smell different," she said. "Don't they? Wasn't that the way you told?"

Weigand nodded, and said they did.

"But not much," he said. "It's not a difference you—well, remember. If you thought you were using kerosene and it was really gasoline your memory of the way kerosene smells wouldn't hold over; you'd just accept the gasoline smell as a kerosene smell. Particularly if you had just got up and were a little fuzzy, as most people are in the morning. Right?"

Mrs. North said she supposed so.

"Well," Weigand said, "what would happen if you poured gasoline on embers?"

"It wouldn't explode?" Mrs. North asked, doubtfully. Weigand said it wouldn't. "Then it would burn up suddenly?" Mrs. North said. Weigand shook his head, and said that was the funny part. Probably it wouldn't.

"Probably," he said, "it would put the embers out." The Norths looked at him, incredulous. "Just that," he said. "The embers would turn black—probably nothing else would happen. But, unless you were trying to you probably wouldn't hit all the embers directly; there would be coals smoldering on the bottom sides of logs, for example. If there were coals still smoldering, nothing would happen for a few seconds, while the gasoline vaporized—it vaporizes much more rapidly than kerosene—and got hot. There might be time enough, for example, to take the can back into the still-room at the Corbin cabin and put it down and come back and sit in front of the fire. Then—well, when it got hot enough, it would puff. It would be a puff almost like an explosion and—"

"But that's only what kerosene does," Mrs. North objected.

Weigand nodded.

"It's precisely what kerosene does, in theory," he said. "But if you used as much gasoline as you would normally use kerosene, it wouldn't be any little tame puff. It would come out in a sheet of fire, spread— well, feet into the room. And if you were sitting on a bench close to the fire, as Jean probably was—" He paused. "Well, you can see how it would be," he said.

Mrs. North drew a gasping breath.

"Oh," she said. "Oh! Not like that!"

"Yes," Weigand said, and there was gentleness in his voice. "I'm afraid just like that. And if there weren't embers to touch it off, and the fireplace was warm, the same thing would happen if you tossed a lighted match into the smoke. The fire would wrap itself around you, and if you were wearing, say, a light, fluffy polo coat over a nightgown—" He seemed to have finished, but after a moment he spoke again. "Well," he said, "that was what Jean Corbin was wearing. And I think that was what happened. Heimrich isn't so sure."

They looked at Heimrich, who was slowly nodding his head.

"It might have been that way," he said. "It's a reconstruction. And if it was that way?"

"You see it," Weigand said. "It was an accident—somehow she got gasoline instead of kerosene—or somebody planned it. And we've had a killing already."

"So," Heimrich said. "Yes, I think so. I wanted to hear you prove it."

"Yes," Weigand said. "I knew that was the idea. Now let's see if the Norths know anything about the can."

Heimrich yelled, suddenly, "Pete!" Everybody looked at him in astonishment, including Pete. Pete looked a little hurt and went over to this strange, odd-smelling man who suddenly called his name. Heimrich looked at Pete in mild surprise. A trooper stuck his head in the door and said, "Yes, Lieutenant?"

"Get the can, Pete," the lieutenant said, and everybody subsided, except the feline Pete, who looked more puzzled than ever. Heimrich looked a little puzzled, too.

"It's his name, too," Mrs. North explained, pointing. Heimrich laughed, suddenly. Trooper Pete came to the door carrying a can.

"Hey," Lieutenant Heimrich said, "you're named after a cat, trooper." The trooper looked startled, and went away when Heimrich waved. They looked at the can.

"Ever see it before?" Weigand said. The Norths looked at it again.

"Is that the one?" Mrs. North said, and then said, "Oh, yes, of course."

"Why 'of course'?" Weigand asked. Mrs. North pointed to a splash of paint on the top of the can.

"That," she said, "I remember noticing it last week. When Jean was making the fire."

"Good girl," Weigand said. "I hoped somebody might."

"It would have been better," Heimrich pointed out, "if she remembered seeing it somewhere else. That would get us somewhere."

That, Weigand agreed, would have been very nice. "But too much to hope," he added, and Heimrich nodded and said, "Oh, yes."

"But look," Mrs. North said. "You mean somebody poured the kerosene out of the can and put in gasoline, knowing it would puff out and burn Jean to death? You mean there's anybody like that—?" She drew closer to her husband, who put an arm around her. "And right after Helen," Mrs. North went on. She started and sat straight. "You think she could have known who killed Helen and had to be—got out of the way?" she said.

There was a little pause, broken by Heimrich.

"That's the way it looks," he said. "It's a hell of a thing."

Weigand hesitated a moment longer.

"Yes," he said, "that's the way it looks. But it doesn't follow that the murderer thought she would burn to death." They looked at him.

"He might, you see, have thought the can would explode while she was holding it," he said. "As you two did. And then she might have died quickly. And then the can would have been gone, and the gasoline, and we would have had mighty little to go on."

Heimrich nodded.

"We haven't too much as it is," he said, "but that would have made it harder. It would have been hard to prove it wasn't some sort of a funny accident. This way—" he paused.

"Well," he said, "this way we can be pretty sure that the same guy got her as got Helen Wilson. We can be pretty sure that she saw something that it wasn't healthy to see and—" But he saw Weigand shaking his head and stopped.

"You could be jumping," he said. He smiled, rather grimly. "Maybe," he said, "somebody just jammed into line out of turn. It could be that way, too."

• 6 •

SUNDAY
11 A.M. TO 11:45 A.M.

Lieutenant Heimrich got up and began to walk back and forth across the room. He walked heavily, with a kind of hard, almost angry, determination. The Norths and Weigand watched him and after a while Weigand spoke. His tone was sympathetic.

"It makes a nice one, doesn't it, Heimrich?" he said. "It all adds up to a straw-stack with a couple of needles in it."

Heimrich said, "Yeh." Then he stopped and stared at Weigand. He looked at him for almost a minute, which is a long time to be looked at.

"Yes?" Weigand said. He said it suspiciously.

"I was just thinking," Heimrich said. "You sound as if you were leaving it in my lap, just like that. You weren't planning to be going anywhere, were you?"

"Now, listen," Weigand said. "I'm on vacation. I'm a city cop. Why should I be taking on this county's headaches? I stopped here for the weekend, planning to drive on into New England and look at trees. Just look at trees; standing around, changing color, not getting into anything. So tomorrow I'm going on and look at some trees."

Heimrich looked at him and said, "Yeah?"

"Damn it all," said Weigand. His voice was, for him, a little blustery, and a smile began to form on Mrs. North's lips. Weigand saw the smile. "Damn it all," he said, more firmly than ever. "Do I ask the State cops to give me a hand in town? Do I?"

Heimrich caught Mrs. North's smile too. She was suddenly conscious that Lieutenant Heimrich was not a man you could count out in such matters. Weigand looked at the two of them.

"Sure you don't," Heimrich said. "Only did I ever find a body in your town? Was I ever all tied up in it? Was I ever—well, say, a material witness? But who said you had to do anything?"

Weigand looked at the three of them, and he tried to look angry. But he knew, as he had known for some time, that he wasn't going on into New England, trees or no trees.

"Truck-driver's," said Mrs. North, unexpectedly.

Heimrich looked at her, baffled. Weigand and Mr. North looked at each other and then Mr. North said, "Oh, yes.

"Bus," he said. "For 'truck' read 'bus.'"

Mrs. North looked at them both and said she was getting sort of tired of them doing that. But she did not speak as if she were really getting sort of tired of it.

"Anyway," she said, "that's the kind of holiday you've worked up for yourself, Mr. Weigand."

Weigand raised both hands a few inches and shrugged, the palms open.

"Right," he said. "I wouldn't buck the law. But it's your case, all the same."

"I wasn't giving you the case," Heimrich said. "So. A little cooperation?"

Weigand nodded. All at once he found he was thinking of Dorian Hunt, and of how lightly she moved. Even with murders, Lone Lake had its points. He looked at the Norths, and asked if they didn't have to get back to town.

"No," Mr. North said. "We were staying through the week, anyhow. A last fling at summer; that sort of thing. So that's all right."

Heimrich walked a minute or two longer, and then he sat down, heavily. But there was, Mrs. North thought, nothing really heavy about his eyes.

"So," he said. "That's fixed. Now where are we?"

Weigand said that where they were was in a mess. At the start of a mess. They had two murders, for all practical purposes simultaneously. They had one method and— "Have we got a medical on Wilson?" he said. Heimrich yelled for Pete, and the cat looked at him disgustedly and did nothing. Trooper Pete appeared.

"Get in touch with the medical examiner's office," Heimrich directed, "and ask them where the hell's the medical on Wilson."

"It's right here," Pete said. "They just sent it. I was just coming along with it."

They took the report and spread it out on the table, Weigand and Heimrich studying it. Mrs. North started to look over Weigand's shoulder, and then decided not to. It was not a long report. Helen Wilson had been about twenty-six, white and female. She had died from a stab wound in the throat, made by a heavy, not very sharp weapon which had torn as much as cut, and severed an artery. She had lost consciousness almost at once and died within a few minutes. When her body was examined—at around 2 A.M.—she had been dead between two and four hours. Making allowances for the coolness of the night and other external conditions, the physician who had performed the autopsy was willing to guess that she had died around eleven o'clock.

Weigand and Heimrich looked at each other. Weigand shook his head.

"As I told you earlier," he said, "I wasn't noticing. I thought I was on vacation. She was at the party for a while and then I noticed that she had gone, but I can't guess about times. Not for her or for anyone. Maybe the Norths?"

The Norths looked at each other and shook their heads.

"I remember talking to her a while after we got there," Mrs. North said. "And seeing her dancing a little later. But I wasn't thinking about times."

Weigand looked at Mr. North and Mr. North shook his head.

"So," said Heimrich. "Suppose we say that the Doc is right. Call it eleven o'clock. Where was the Corbin girl then, does anybody know?"

Nobody did. She had been with Weigand for about half an hour, he guessed, before he walked back with her to her cabin. Say he could account for her from 12:30 on. Before that he'd seen her once or twice, but couldn't say when.

"And she didn't act as if she knew anything then, obviously," Heimrich said. "Or you'd have said so."

"As far as I know she acted normally," Weigand said. "I didn't have much chance to know what normal was for her, of course. But I'd be pretty sure she hadn't witnessed a murder."

"But—" Heimrich began.

Weigand said, "Right. She didn't need to see it, I agree. She might have seen something else that meant nothing at the time, but might have meant a lot after Helen's body was found. Somebody carrying something, perhaps. The weapon—what the hell *was* the weapon?"

All four of them shook their heads, the Norths in sympathy with the detectives.

"So—" said Heimrich, after a pause. "It leaves things open. The Corbin girl may have seen something which made her dangerous to the man who killed Wilson, if it was a man. And then while the party was going on he may have sneaked out, substituted gasoline for kerosene, and waited for things to happen. As they did. So if we find out who killed Helen Wilson, and why, we'll know who killed Jean Corbin."

"Right," Weigand said. "And go on."

Heimrich looked at him, inquiringly. Weigand said there was no good his pretending he didn't see the rest of it. That it worked the other way, just as well.

"We don't know when the gasoline was substituted," he said. "It might have been almost any time yesterday. Helen Wilson may have stumbled on something about the substitution which would be dangerous to the murderer after the Corbin girl was dead and Helen began remembering. So the murderer may have persuaded her to leave the party and then killed her so she couldn't talk later. In that case, if we find out who killed Jean Corbin, we'll know who killed Helen Wilson."

"That," Heimrich said, "certainly tangles it up nice."

"But listen—" said Mrs. North, out of the ensuing pause. "It could have been both—together, I mean. It doesn't have to be first one and then the other."

"But it *was* first one and then the other," Heimrich said. "It was first Helen Wilson between ten and midnight and then Jean Corbin a little after eight. So—" His voice trailed off, as a thought struck him. He looked at Mrs. North with something approaching animus.

"Yes," said Weigand, "she would bring that up. But we've got to consider it. There may have been one motive covering both girls, so that the order of the murders doesn't mean a thing. Maybe neither was killed because she knew something about the murder of the other, but because the murderer had a motive to kill both."

"That helps," Heimrich said, and got up and began to walk the floor again. "And there may have been two murderers. And the Corbin girl's death may have been an accident we haven't doped out. The whole damn thing may be a coincidence. That certainly helps."

"Well," Weigand said, "we don't have to take on all the possibilities at once. That's something. And I doubt whether accident or coincidence come into it. It doesn't look that way now, anyway."

"Yeh," Heimrich said. "And we'd better get at it. We've got to find the weapon that killed Wilson. Maybe we can trace the gasoline in the Corbin oil-can. Maybe somebody bought it."

"It's more likely somebody siphoned it out of a car," Weigand pointed out. Heimrich said sure it was, but they'd have to check.

"I've got men dragging the lake, of course," he said. "I'll get men checking on sales of gasoline and—" He broke off, considering. Then he shook his head. "I was wondering if we could check car tanks, someway," he said. "Find out when the tanks of the various cars were filled last, how far the cars have been driven, what they burn per mile and how much is left. But that would just drive us crazy—nobody'd know whether their last purchase filled their tank, or where they'd been since. We'll have to get it some other way. Maybe somebody did just walk into a filling station with a two-gallon can and have it filled up."

Weigand and Heimrich looked at each other. Neither looked hopeful.

"Prints we're getting from the Corbin can," Heimrich went on, "and we'll pick up prints around camp." He thought. "Do you think of anything else?" he asked Weigand.

Weigand thought of two points and ticked them off. One, find out whether anybody at Lone Lake had recently bought a new, two-gallon kerosene can. Two, find out who had bought kerosene the day before. "At Ireland's?" he questioned the Norths. They nodded.

"Everybody does," Mrs. North said. "He keeps it in a lean-to, locked up. We bought some yesterday. Why?"

Weigand said that knowing might come in useful.

"But why the new can?" North asked, and Heimrich looked interested, too. Weigand said that somebody had to have an extra can, obviously, and if he didn't already have a spare he'd have to get one.

"Any other course would be too risky," Weigand added.

North and Heimrich looked at each other, now. "Cryptic, that's what these people are," North said. "Comes from associating with my wife. Maybe I'd better look into it?"

"Well," Heimrich said, "I don't get it. Somebody took a can of gasoline to the Corbin cabin, poured it into the can there, took it away again. Where's your third can?"

"Wait a minute!" Mrs. North said. "I'm getting it, sort of. Was there kerosene already in her can?"

That, Weigand said, was precisely what they had to consider. Possibly they could find out, someway. No—wait a minute.

"We know there must have been some kerosene in the can," he said, "because she used it. That is—she thought she was using it. If the can had been empty she would never have tried to pour from it to start the fire. And—this isn't so certain—it probably was full during the day, before the murderer made the switch, because it's full now. If it were only half-full when the switch was made it would be only half-full now, unless the murderer was pretty dim-witted."

"Why?" said Mr. North, dimly.

"So it would weigh approximately what she expected when she picked it up," Weigand pointed out. "She might not have noticed the difference, but the chances are at least even she would have, and anybody thinking about it would know that. He'd want to have the same weight of gasoline she would expect of kerosene. Right?"

"Of course," said Mrs. North. "Anybody could see that." She looked at Mr. North pityingly.

"And," she said, "if the can was full when he—the murderer, I mean—got there he'd have to have three cans. Or something else. To pour into."

"Look," said Mr. North, "you've got me all mixed up. Do you see it, Heimrich?"

"Yes," Heimrich said. "They've got something there."

Mrs. North said that Jerry wasn't being as bright as she'd hoped and it made one wonder.

"A fool's paradise," she said. "That's where I've been living. Look—"

You went with a full can of gasoline, holding two gallons, to substitute it for kerosene in another can which, as they had demonstrated, was almost certainly full or nearly full. You couldn't merely switch the cans, because one could be identified. So you had to have a third can, or some other receptacle, to pour the kerosene into while—

"Oh, of course," said Mr. North. "Only why not just pour it out? Or why not just use a pan from the kitchen?"

"Well—" said Mrs. North and looked doubtful for a moment. "You tell him, Bill," she said.

"Take the last possibility first," Weigand suggested. "It would smell up the pan. She might use the pan for cooking, or start to, before she used the gasoline. It might make her suspicious. Throwing it away has several disadvantages from the murderer's viewpoint, depending on where he threw it. If he poured it down the sink in the kitchen, it would smell. If he poured it near the house it would smell. But if he went around looking for a secluded place far enough away, he would increase the chances of being noticed—and being noticed while doing something odd. If he poured it nearby, taking a chance on the odor it would—"

"Leave a mark," Mrs. North said. "Kill the grass."

Weigand nodded.

"If he carried it down to the lake and poured it in, it would leave an oil scum," he said. "And why do any of these things? Why not just take it home in his own can and use it up?"

"Well—" said Mr. North, "that sounds sensible."

Heimrich nodded.

"So—" he said. "It's worth playing it that way until we find out different. So we'll check on cans and kerosene too. Meanwhile, we'd better ask some questions."

They asked their questions, and were at it until well into the evening, with one or two interruptions. And afterward Weigand and Heimrich agreed they hadn't been very bright about it, because at least once they had had their fingers on something and let it get away. They had an ugly reason to be sure of that, as it turned out, because the murderer they were after saw what they failed to see and acted, quickly and ruthlessly, on what he saw.

· 7 ·

SUNDAY
11:45 A.M. TO 1:10 P.M.

The two detectives, with Heimrich doing most of the talking, started their questioning in the Norths' living-room and allowed the Norths to remain, although Heimrich looked rather doubtful when this was decided and pointed out that he planned to do the talking. They thought of rounding everybody up for a general interrogation, and abandoned that plan. Instead, the various people who had been at the Fullers' party, and the half-dozen who had not, were severally summoned to the Norths' cabin by troopers, talked to and sent home.

The Fullers came first and, separately, outlined their day. It turned out to be a day characteristic of many. They had driven up to camp the evening before, had a few drinks with the Norths that evening and slept late. Jane Fuller had cooked the breakfast, the Fullers had eaten it, Ben Fuller had washed up. They had cleaned the cabin and filled the lamps and then had driven, together, to Danbury to lay in liquor and other supplies for the party. They had got in a set of tennis early in the afternoon, while the light was still bad for the tournament. Then they had watched the mixed double finals, stopped at the Norths' for drinks afterward, had a light dinner and then had their party which lasted until the body of Helen Wilson had been found. After that, as their guardian trooper could testify, they had talked a while and gone to bed. Neither knew any motive anyone might have for killing Helen Wilson; neither could cite a specific motive for the murder of Jean Corbin, but both agreed, when Weigand asked them, that the second death was less surprising than the first.

Mrs. Evelyn Abel had gone home after the tournament match, although her husband had stopped at Van Horst's with some others for a drink. She had been feeling headachy all day and had taken some aspirin and lain down. She had felt better in the evening and had gone to the party with her husband and had been just about to go home when Helen Wilson's body had been found. She had been out of the cabin once during the party, but she could only guess that the time was a little before midnight.

"I went to—" she said, and stopped.

"Right," Weigand said. "We've learned that the cabins haven't indoor toilet facilities, Mrs. Abel."

"Well," she said, "that was it. That's the only time I was out."

She had liked Helen Wilson.

"And Jean Corbin?" Weigand asked.

"Oh, yes," Evelyn Abel said, very brightly, very quickly. "She was a charming girl."

"So—" Heimrich said, and thanked her.

Dr. Abel was precise of speech and thought, and his account of their day paralleled that of his wife, except that he had stopped at Van Horst's for a drink after the tennis and gone home to find Mrs. Abel lying down. He had been out of the Fuller cabin once or twice during the party, "for obvious reasons," he added, but could not guess about the time. He had known Helen Wilson only slightly.

"And Miss Corbin?" Weigand broke in.

"Yes," he said, "I knew her rather better. I had taken her to lunch in town once or twice."

"That was all?" Weigand said.

"Certainly." Dr. Abel seemed surprised. Then he smiled, a little frostily.

"Were you led to believe there was more?" he asked. He seemed amused. He looked at the Norths, sitting side by side on the couch, and his smile did not lose its frost. Mrs. North flushed and started to speak.

"Why—" she said, but Weigand motioned her to quiet and then she said: "Ouch!

"Don't pinch me," she said, indignantly, to Mr. North. "I wasn't going to say anything."

Dr. Abel, sitting in angular ease in a chair near the fireplace, seemed to be enjoying something. When he spoke, enjoyment leaked from his voice, although his words were commonplace enough.

"You gentlemen will not, I am sure, be influenced by gossip," he said. "Particularly when you can prove nothing."

"So," Heimrich said. "That will be all, thank you, Professor."

Abel was a tall, thin man when he stood, and there was detached assurance in his manner.

"I wish you luck, gentlemen," he said, and went out of the cabin, squinting against the sun.

"Listen!" said Mrs. North. "He's pulling wool. Jean Corbin was making a play for him, whatever he says. And Evelyn Abel knew it, whatever she says. Did you notice the way she acted?"

"Yes," Weigand said. "We noticed it. But you mustn't break in, Pam."

Mrs. North said, a little indignantly, that she hadn't been going to.

"But just the same," she said, "you ought to watch that man. He'd just as soon kill anybody as not, if they got in his way, or bothered him. He'd just—brush them off."

Heimrich and Weigand looked at each other and after a while Weigand nodded.

"Yes," he said. "Yes, I think that's quite possibly true, in a sense. Don't you?"

"So—" Heimrich said. "So."

He sent a trooper for Dorian Hunt, and Weigand felt a kind of eagerness which surprised him. Dorian came after a little and stood for just a moment framed by the sunlight in the door. She looked at the detectives dispassionately, without friendliness. She smiled at the Norths, faintly, briefly, and sat where Weigand motioned her to sit. The motion of her sitting was smooth and fluid. She waited, unhurried and alert. She shook her head when Weigand offered her a cigarette, and sat waiting.

She sat quietly, for the most part, with brown legs crossed and one foot swinging. The short skirt of her dark green frock was only a subterfuge of a skirt, falling open as she sat, to reveal creased green shorts under it. She was a little paler than she had been the day before, Weigand thought, and there were faint freckles on her cheekbones. Her eyes could not, obviously, really have a greenish tint—that must be a reflection from her dress. But there was, as he had remembered, red in her hair when the sun caught it. The sun caught it now, streaming through the door behind her. And there was something about her which made Weigand feel that he had seen her before, under different circumstances and far from Lone Lake. But he could not remember what it was; possibly, he thought, with a sudden start, he had only wanted to see her before.

She had come up the night before, by a late train with Helen Wilson. That morning, after breakfast, she had gone for a walk, alone, and then she had sat on the Wilson porch and talked with Helen and Arthur Kennedy before lunch. It had been a late lunch and afterward they had watched the tennis most of the afternoon.

"Except when I was up here," she said. Later they had had dinner—Helen and her mother, Arthur Kennedy and Thelma Smith, who had come up that morning and been met at the train by Helen and Kennedy. Then she had gone to the party with the others, except Mrs. Wilson.

"Now," said Heimrich, "can you remember anything specific about the party? How long Helen was there, for example; when you first missed her? Did you leave the house yourself, by the way?"

"Yes," Dorian said. "I left once, I think, I don't know what time. Helen was there when I came back, I know, and a little later she was dancing and passed near and smiled at me. But I can't remember times." She looked at Weigand. "You were there," she said. "You're a detective. Why don't you remember?"

"Well," Weigand said, "I wasn't a detective at the time, apparently. And most of the people were still strange to me, and distracting."

Dorian pointed out that most of them were strange to her, too.

"And I'm not a detective," she said. "Thank God."

"Right," Weigand said. He felt a little nonplused for a moment.

"It isn't necessary that you like this, Miss Hunt," he said, finally. "It isn't necessary that you like us. But we're hunting for a person who killed your friend. We're trying to find out who, and why. It would seem to me that you would want to help."

The swinging brown leg swung more quickly; stopped swinging with the toe caught tensely against the floor.

"Helen was my friend," the girl said, and her voice was without expression. "There's nothing to do about that. I'll tell you what I know, but I won't—help hunt." She stopped suddenly and looked at Weigand. "I've seen hunting," she said. "I've seen men hunting a—" She broke off. "Other things," she said, but it was not what she had intended to say.

"Do you know any reason why somebody should want to kill your friend?" Heimrich asked.

"No."

"Or Jean Corbin?"

"I barely knew her," Dorian said. "How would I know what people felt about her?"

Weigand watched her and something came back, vaguely, uncertainly. He had seen her before and, gropingly, he went back into his memory. There was a chair and a light shining on it from behind and one crossed leg was swinging nervously. Then he had it, and he looked at Dorian Hunt gently, almost anxiously.

"Are you Clayton Hunt's daughter?" he asked. The leg swung quickly, then paused.

"Why should you think I'm Clayton Hunt's daughter?" she asked. "It's a common name, isn't it?"

"Yes," Weigand said. "It's a common name. Are you Clayton Hunt's daughter?"

She stared back at him.

"All right," she said. "Clayton Hunt is my father. So what now? Haven't you done enough to us?"

Her voice was higher. It did not shake, but it seemed as if it might break.

"I'm not trying to do anything to you, Miss Hunt," Weigand said. He felt Heimrich and the Norths looking at him, expectantly. "I just remembered. You testified for him and I happened to be in the courtroom. It wasn't my case, you understand. I had nothing to do with it."

"Well," the girl said, "what has it got to do with this? Except to bring it all back—to make me conscious of it again?"

Weigand said that he didn't know it had anything to do with it, but Heimrich said, "What's all this?"

"I'll tell him!" Dorian said. She said it bitterly. "My father was Clayton Hunt. Didn't you read about it? Everybody else read about it. He was a broker and everybody thought he was fine—he was fine. But then he lost, and borrowed on securities friends had let him have and—and they hunted him, and closed in on him and said he was a thief. And they sent him to prison. Is that what you want to know?"

"Oh," Heimrich said. "That Hunt. Yes, I remember. I'm—I'm sorry about it."

"Why," the girl said, "should you be sorry about it? Nobody asked you to be sorry about it."

There was something else about the case, Weigand was thinking. It had been, from her side, as she told it. Everybody had thought highly of Clayton Hunt. He had been on many boards, some of them charitable. And he had—if you wanted to call it that—"borrowed" on securities entrusted to him, in one or two cases by the boards and in one case by the board of one of the charities. Probably he had meant to repay. But he didn't repay. And so he was in Sing Sing. But there had been something else.

"When did you meet Helen Wilson?" he asked, suddenly. Dorian looked at him, and she looked as if she hated him.

"About four years ago," she said.

"Was she with the advertising agency then, do you remember?" he asked.

"No."

"Wasn't she the secretary—?"

The girl broke in.

"All right," she said. "Hunt and dig and hurt people. All right. She was my father's secretary. They made her testify against him. They said awful things about her and about him and they weren't true. Nobody thought they were true, but he was down—and we were down. So it was great fun for the papers."

Weigand remembered, now, although there was no image with his memory—only a name. Helen Wilson. She had, reluctantly, testified for the State; she had tried to minimize what they made her tell, tried to make it sound better. They hadn't let her. And one of the newspapers had tried to twist her evident regard and respect for Clayton Hunt into something else—hinting, half-saying, printing lines meant to be read between.

"She came to us," Dorian said. "To Mother and me, before Mother died—before it killed her. She didn't want us to believe what they said—she wanted us to know that Father was as fine with her as he always was."

"You believed her?" Heimrich asked.

She looked at him.

"What would *you* know about a man like Father?" she said. Her voice was dull, rather hopeless. "Of course we believed her—we knew him. She was just another person who had suffered; who had been caught, as he was and we were, by the hunters—tracking him down, twisting what he did—"

Suddenly the reddish brown hair was down against an arm of the green suit, and she was sobbing. Mrs. North knelt beside her and put an arm about her shoulders and glared at the detectives. She glared at him as much as at Heimrich, Weigand was disturbed to notice.

"Damn you both," Mrs. North said. "Leave her alone—you—you *men*!"

Weigand felt a little embarrassed and, looking at Heimrich, he saw that Heimrich apparently felt the same. Mr. North too, he imagined. Mrs. North looked at them angrily, and drew Dorian to her feet.

"You're going to leave her alone," she said. "You've asked her all you're going to ask. I'm—I'm taking her riding."

Dorian Hunt straightened a little when the two went out. But she did not look back, and she let Mrs. North guide her.

"Riding?" Heimrich said.

Mr. North nodded.

"It's Pam's remedy," he said. "When people are troubled, take them somewhere in a car. I wouldn't try to stop them."

"No," Weigand said. "I think he's right about that."

There was the grind of a starter and the roar of a motor as it caught and raced. The gears meshed with an angry snarl.

"She always does that," Mr. North said. "Particularly when she's in a hurry. I can't think why."

The motor snorted and died. It started more angrily than ever. The gears snarled again. The motor coughed and settled into its stride.

"They're gone," Mr. North said. "Unless she hit something getting out. Will one of you look?"

They were gone, Weigand discovered. There was what looked, from the distance, like a streak of green paint on one of the gate-stones and it looked as if a green car—about the color of the Norths'—had left it. But Weigand decided not to mention that.

"So," Heimrich said as Weigand turned back into the room, and felt that it was peculiarly emptier than it had been.

"So?" Weigand said.

"Would it be a motive if Miss Hunt thought the Wilson girl had helped send her father up?" he inquired. "Particularly if she didn't believe that everything was innocent between her father and the Wilson girl? Could Miss Hunt merely have pretended to believe that everything was innocent and waited her time?"

"Well," Weigand said, "it could be argued that way, I suppose. She obviously feels deeply about her father—maybe she isn't very balanced when that subject comes up. Only—"

"Only?" Heimrich mimicked.

"Right," Weigand said. "I won't say it."

Heimrich said he wouldn't. She seemed like a nice girl, sure. She didn't look like a murderer, she looked—

"Sunny," Weigand said, to his own surprise.

All right, Heimrich would agree, she didn't look the part. And had all the murderers of Weigand's acquaintance looked the part? Weigand told him to skip it.

"I tell you what it is," Heimrich said. "We don't know anything about these people. Where they come from, what they are—this goes back into the past. Tangles we don't know about. Relationships—"

"Right," Weigand said. "Nobody's stopping us. We'll find out. Who do you want to work on next?"

Heimrich thumbed his list and said they might as well finish the people at the Wilson house. Kennedy, say.

Kennedy looked like a recent Princeton graduate. He was a recent Princeton graduate, now working in Wall Street. He had spent the day before in utter innocence, driving with Helen to meet Thelma Smith; lunching, watching the tennis, going home afterward to mix a cocktail for Mrs. Wilson and sit soberly on the porch with her, discussing his mother's friends. Mrs. Wilson had grown up with some of his mother's friends. Then he had gone to the party, and the time he had had couldn't have been better until the end, which couldn't have been more horrifying.

He knew the Wilsons through his family; more precisely, knew Mrs. Wilson through his family. He had seen very little of any of them, however, until a few months earlier. He had been at school and everything. He had met Helen for the first time the winter before. The families had drifted apart when Mrs. Wilson married the second time and when Helen came into the family and—

"Came into the family?" Heimrich asked, puzzled.

"Perhaps I phrase that badly," he said. "But she's Mrs. Wilson's stepdaughter, you know, not her own daughter."

The two detectives looked at each other.

"Well," Heimrich said. "That's the first—" He broke off at a shake of Weigand's head.

"Thank you, Mr. Kennedy," Weigand said. "I take it you know of no reason for Helen Wilson's murder? Or Jean Corbin's?"

Kennedy shook his head.

"Right," Weigand said. "I think that will be all, for now."

Kennedy went out, looking relieved. Heimrich started to speak.

"Right," Weigand said. "But let's get it from Mrs. Wilson, shall we? We're getting too much second-hand, as it is."

Heimrich thought a moment, and nodded.

"Send for her?" he asked. "Or—?"

Weigand thought that, under the circumstances, they might go down to the Wilson house. Heimrich nodded again. When they started they did not invite Mr. North to go with them, but he decided they had not invited him to stay behind. So he followed along. It was getting interesting, he decided.

The path from the front door half circled the house, passing close to the open kitchen window. They had passed it when Mr. North saw something and stopped. The others stopped and he pointed.

"Somebody throwing lighted cigarettes in the grass," he said. "It's too dry for that. Risky. I'll just stamp it out."

A thin twist of smoke was rising from the grass where he pointed and he moved toward it.

Weigand said: "Wait a minute.

"Neither of you threw it, did you?" he asked. "Pam and Miss Hunt didn't come this way. Kennedy didn't and the others have been gone too long. So unless some of your troopers have been sneaking a drag, Heimrich—"

Heimrich called the two troopers who had been waiting on the other side, down by the stone wall, to act as messengers. He said he would forget any infraction of regulations, this time. He just wanted to know. Had either of them been smoking near the house and thrown a lighted cigarette away? They were both firm in denials.

"So—" Heimrich said.

"Right," said Weigand. "It looks as if somebody had been standing here listening. Now, I wonder what he wanted to hear?"

He went over to pick up the cigarette, but there was nothing left to pick up—only a gray ash, toward the end of which a coal was dying.

"Well," Weigand said, "that's one we won't find lipstick on. Or anything else." He looked at Heimrich. "It looks as if we haven't been very careful, mister," he said. "I wonder if whoever it was heard anything he wanted to know?"

• 8 •

SUNDAY
1:10 P.M. TO 2:20 P.M.

The path they followed dipped toward the tennis courts and then, a little beyond them, forked off to the left from the path which Weigand
remembered as leading to the shower. It came out of the prevailing
sumach into a field which was occupied by a fat man in his sixties clad
in an undershirt and, precariously, in trousers. He was sending a scythe
swishing through the tall grass in a movement which appeared, from a
little distance, to be effortless. But as they neared, he rested the scythe
on the ground and mopped his head with a blue handkerchief.

"Hot," he announced.

"Looks it," Mr. North agreed. "Hiya, Mr. Marvin."

Mr. Marvin grunted, and repeated that he was hot. He looked at the
two men with Mr. North and grunted again.

"See you got some friends, Jerry," he said. "Hear you've been having some doin's around here, ain't you?"

He spoke of the "doin's" with a kind of pleased relish.

"I guess these must be the detectives I been hearin' about," he said,
pushing the handkerchief back into his pocket with a force which,

61

under the circumstances, was clearly foolhardy. "These gentlemen the detectives, Jerry?"

Mr. North said that that was right.

"Lieutenant Heimrich," he said. "Lieutenant Weigand."

Marvin shook hands damply.

"Glad to meet you, gentlemen," he said. "From what I hear around they sorta got you stumped."

He laughed a subterranean rumble, and turned on Mr. North a wink that seemed to dislocate his face.

"This is Mr. Henry Marvin, Bill, Heimrich," Mr. North said. "Mr. Marvin has a farm on the other side of the valley. Now and then he helps out around the lake. Sort of gives Van Horst a hand when he needs it. Isn't that right, Mr. Marvin?"

Mr. Marvin said it was, and looked mysterious. He looked around and saw no one.

"Van ain't no hand with a scythe," he said. "That's why I have to give him a hand. There ain't many around here nowadays who know how to use a scythe."

He demonstrated that he was one of that limited number, sending the scythe whispering through the grass. The grass fell, cut clean as by a mower and hardly higher above the ground's surface.

"Takes practice," Mr. Marvin admitted. "Wait till I get my beer."

He hitched his trousers and lumbered to a patch of shade. He uncapped a bottle, lifted it and the liquid bumped out of the bottle into Mr. Marvin, leaving only foam behind. Mr. Marvin wiped his mouth with the blue handkerchief and returned. He said there was nothing like beer.

"Give me beer any day," he said. "There's some around here who drink apple right through the summer, but me and beer get along all right. You can give me beer."

He looked at Mr. North as he repeated his offer. Mr. North nodded, and said he thought there were a couple of bottles on ice, if Mr. Marvin wanted to get them. Mr. Marvin said he wasn't like some people. He didn't have to have it on ice.

"Just so as it's beer," he said. He picked up the scythe, apparently ending the discussion. The two detectives and Mr. North started to walk on. Mr. Marvin let them walk a few yards and then he said, "Hey." They paused and he said, "Come back here a minute." They hesitated and went back, North and Weigand looking a little amused. Heimrich looked impatient. Mr. Marvin said he would tell them how it was.

"You gentlemen look all right to me," Mr. Marvin said. "I might give you a hand. Just keep an eye on this Mr. Van Horst of yours."

He then returned to scything, with an air of accomplishment complete. Heimrich started to speak, but Mr. North shook his head and touched the State Police lieutenant on the arm.

"How's that, Mr. Marvin?" he asked. "I've been telling these gentlemen they ought to come to you if they wanted facts. I told them you knew more about the people around here than all the rest of us put together."

"You was right, Jerry," Mr. Marvin admitted. "You was right, all right."

"About Van Horst?" North suggested.

Mr. Marvin put down his scythe again, and said he wanted it understood that Van was a friend of his. He said he wouldn't give a hand to anybody who wasn't a friend of his, because fifty cents an hour was just about not worth the trouble. But Jerry was a friend of his, too. "Ain't that right?" he asked Mr. North, and Mr. North said it certainly was. Mr. Marvin said he wouldn't say anything to get anybody in trouble, because he didn't hold with getting people into trouble, and Mr. North said he knew just how Mr. Marvin felt.

"All right," Mr. Marvin said. "You just ask Van about his wife."

Mr. North looked authentically surprised.

"His wife?" he repeated. "Van hasn't got a wife."

Mr. Marvin looked at him, consideringly, and then began to nod, slowly, meaningfully.

"That's what I say," he said. "He ain't got a wife. But that ain't saying he didn't *have* a wife, is it? You bet it ain't. Seven-eight years ago, when he first came, he had a wife, all right. One of these women in pants."

He spat.

"Women in pants!" he said. "What do you expect?"

"Mrs. Van Horst," North pressed. "What became of her?"

Mr. Marvin looked at him again, and his look was overflowing with the curd of hidden meaning. He nodded several times, including all three in a gloomy gaze and said that was what a lot of people wondered.

"One week she was here and the next week she wasn't here," he said. "All at once she just wasn't around, in pants or anything. What do you think of that, gentlemen?"

"Well, Mr. Marvin," Mr. North said, "I'd think she went away for some reason."

Mr. Marvin snorted.

"That's what Van was telling people when they asked," he said. "Telling them she just went away." His tone suggested doubt of their belief.

"Well," said Mr. North, "what do they think?"

Mr. Marvin wasn't saying what they thought.

"It ain't for me to tell detectives their business," he said. "I'm just tellin' you what some thought."

He looked at them darkly.

"Get what I mean, don't you?" he said. He paused. "That was when he was livin' in the camp where the Corbin woman lived—the one that got burnt," he said. He grew increasingly portentous. "There was some as figured that if you looked under the floor of that cabin you'd find things," he said. "I ain't making any statements, but that's what some thought." He nodded his head, and then he advanced a step toward the detectives and Mr. North, exhaling beer. *"Maybe that Corbin lady looked!"* he said, and stared at them to further the sinkage of his words. Then he went back to scything and, without looking back, moved away from them along the straight edge of his previous swathe. They looked after him and after a time Mr. North said, reflectively, "Well."

Heimrich snorted, angrily.

"The old loon!" he said.

"Oh," said Mr. North, "do you know Marvin?"

Heimrich said he did.

"Just looking around for killers, I'd pick old Marvin as a likely one," he said. "He pulled a knife on his son-in-law a couple of years ago, you know. Cut him up pretty bad, too, but got off with a jail sentence. Now he's got it in for Van Horst, apparently—I'll pass the word along."

Weigand nodded and said that seemed wise.

"I wonder, though," he said, "whether Van Horst *was* married, and where his wife is now?"

Heimrich walked on a few paces and then he half turned and nodded.

"So—" he said. "We'll have to find out, of course. Just for the record, like."

The path crossed a brook by a wide plank, turned among some lilac bushes and emerged by a cabin. Mr. North said that here was Van Horst's now, if they wanted to talk to him and, when they nodded, yelled, "Van!" Then he yelled again and finally they knocked at the door. But nobody answered, and they followed the path on around Van Horst's cabin until it came out on a grassy plot in front of a rambling frame house, which had obviously been a farmhouse. Arthur Kennedy was sitting on the porch, talking to a comfortable, white-haired woman in her late fifties whose face was pale and rather drawn. They walked on to the porch and North introduced Weigand and Heimrich to Mrs. Wilson.

Mrs. Wilson acknowledged them in a still voice and then, as their presence reminded her, her eyes filled with tears. The detectives and Mr. North waited, and Mr. North wished he had not come. Then Heimrich said that they were very sorry; that whatever they said or did must, obviously, come as an intrusion. But Mrs. Wilson would realize—

She nodded and started to speak in a choked voice, and cleared her throat and spoke again.

"Of course," she said. "I realize that certain things must be done. But there isn't anything I can tell you."

There was little, it seemed, that she could tell them of her daughter's movements the day before; little that they did not already know. The trip to the station to meet Thelma; the luncheon; the tennis match.

"She came back with Dorian a good while after the Askews went by and I knew the game was over," Mrs. Wilson said. "But she said she was at your house, Mr. North?"

Mr. North nodded.

Then they had had dinner, rather late, and Helen, with Arthur Kennedy, Dorian and Thelma had gone to a party at the Fullers'. Thelma had come home early, but the others had not come.

"I would have worried if Arthur and Dorian hadn't been with her," Mrs. Wilson said. "But they were and I didn't worry and then— Then a trooper came and told me."

Her face worked and her voice choked. Heimrich waited.

"Kennedy, here, says she was your stepdaughter, Mrs. Wilson," he said, after the pause.

She nodded and found a handkerchief in her lap and pressed it to her eyes.

"But it didn't make any difference in the way I felt," she said. "She was mine ever since she was a little girl and I loved her as mine. It didn't make any difference."

"No," Heimrich said. "It would be that way. It was—"

But Mrs. Wilson seemed not to hear him, and went on talking as if to herself.

"—she was a little girl with yellow hair and it curled," she said. "And when she was tired she would come up and lean her head against me."

"Yes," Weigand said. "Try not to remember for a little while, Mrs. Wilson."

She seemed not to hear him.

"—and after all that trouble about Mr. Hunt," she said. "And just when it seemed such a wonderful thing was going to happen." She started up, and then sank back again. "It isn't fair," she said. "She was gentle and loved people—"

It was embarrassing to find nothing to say, to know that nothing could be said. Heimrich turned his hat in his hands, twisting its brim. He looked at Weigand and gestured with his head. But Weigand was looking at Mrs. Wilson, pityingly but with speculation.

"What was the wonderful thing, Mrs. Wilson?" he asked. "What was going to happen?"

Mrs. Wilson did not seem to hear him at first, and he waited, without repeating. Then, as if his words had hung until then in the air, she heard and looked at him, as if from a long way off.

"Oh," she said. "I was thinking of the money, and how she could do all the things she had wanted to do—go places and—and everything."

"The money?" Weigand prompted.

She told them, then, haltingly, and from her first words the two detectives were alert, startled. "The Brownley fortune," were her first words, and she hardly needed to go farther. Everybody knew about the Brownley fortune—the fortune which had grown slowly for three generations of sitting tight and holding land; of living tight and hoarding money, until only one strange, crotchety old man was left. And then, in a house near the Hudson at the tip of Manhattan, the old man had died at night, and there had been a great hullabaloo and a scramble. He had been the last of the Brownleys, in direct line, and he had not bothered to make a will because he had not wanted to think of dying, and it made trouble for the surrogate of the county. It made a good story for the newspapers, too, and as the story spread there had been Brownleys nobody had dreamed of in the most out-of-the-way bushes. But, so far as Weigand could remember, there had as yet been no decision; the surrogate was still weeding out claimants, seeking the kin in the nearest degree.

But apparently, if Mrs. Wilson was right, matters had progressed farther than the public knew—had progressed to the point where the principal heir was established. And the principal heir, the next of kin, was Helen Wilson. It would have meant a fortune. How big a fortune no one knew, Mrs. Wilson thought. The newspapers had talked generously of millions, making a good story better, but apparently it was not to be millions. But at the least, and of that the lawyers were sure, it would be a great deal of money; enough money so that Helen Wilson, had she lived a little longer, might have begun to do all the things she had wanted to do since she was a tiny girl with curling yellow hair and old enough to think of beautiful, wonderful things to do.

"And now?" Weigand asked. Did Mrs. Wilson know what happened to the money now?

Now, Mrs. Wilson knew, it went to several distant Brownleys who were kin in the fifth degree, to be divided among them. She had heard Helen and Johnny Blair talking about it and Blair had laughed and told her to watch out she wasn't ganged on, because it was a lot of money.

"Blair?" Weigand said. "Why Blair?"

Mrs. Wilson looked at him, puzzled, and then her face cleared and she said it was stupid of her, and of course there was no reason he should know.

"Johnny is one of the others—the next in line," she said. "He and Helen were some sort of cousins, and—"

But then she broke off and looked at the detectives and a strange expression came over her face.

"No," she said. "Oh no—it couldn't be."

But the first "no" was more assured than the second, and toward the end her voice trailed off.

• 9 •

SUNDAY
2:20 P.M. TO 3:15 P.M.

The two police lieutenants and Mr. North had walked a hundred yards along the path away from the Wilson house before anybody said anything, and then nothing very conclusive was said.

"Well," said Mr. North. He thought it over. "Well," he said.

They went on a little farther.

"I would have thought that Helen Wilson, of all people, was—well, wasn't the sort of person things happen to," Mr. North said. "And now—my God."

Weigand nodded. Things were, he admitted, piling up.

"Listen," he said, to Heimrich. "I thought we were *un*raveling this. I thought we were getting places."

Heimrich's reply was short and emphatic. Then he thought a moment and said that, anyway, they were getting to know where they stood.

"Anyhow," he said, "we're getting the Corbin girl out of it. That's something. We won't have to look hard to find out who killed her, once we find out who killed Helen. That's something."

He said it emphatically; a little too emphatically. He looked at Weigand for agreement. Weigand started to say something and stopped and looked along the path. A man was turning the corner by the Van Horst house.

"Van," Mr. North said. "Want him now?"

The detectives consulted, wordlessly.

"All right," Weigand said. "We'll take him now."

Mr. North yelled, "Hey, Van!" and the man stopped, looked at them a moment and waved. When they came up he agreed to go on to the Norths' cabin and answer a few questions.

"Routine questions, of course?" he said, smiling. "They always are, aren't they?"

"Sure," Heimrich said. "Just routine."

But even routine questions were delayed when they reached the North cabin, because Pam North was back before them. She looked at them without cordiality, and then smiled at Mr. North. Then, after hesitating a moment, she smiled at the others. And however she felt, she had spent her time well.

"Dorian didn't want to come back," she said. "She said she wanted to be alone and walk it off. So I made sandwiches." She looked at them. "Although heaven knows why, for you—you buzzards," she said.

The sandwiches, however, were piled comfortably on a plate and went fine with beer, although when he looked for beer Mr. North snorted. "Marvin took three bottles!" he reported, indignantly. Those that were left, cold, just went around, with the Norths sharing a bottle. Van Horst said he had had lunch, but sat with a beer in one hand and his pipe smoldering in the other, and seemed agreeably at home. They finished and Van Horst said, "Well?"

"We may as well get this out of the way first," Heimrich said. "Are you married?"

Van Horst looked at them in astonishment. Then he looked at the Norths and after a moment smiled, a little crookedly.

"Yes," he said. "I'm married—in a way. Why?"

"You and your wife are separated?" Heimrich asked.

"Obviously."

"And where is she?"

"Just a minute," Van Horst said. "Where is this leading? What has my wife to do with this?"

"Does she live around here?" Heimrich pressed.

"She lives in California," Van Horst said. "And what the hell—?"

Heimrich turned an examining gaze on Van Horst, looked at Weigand for confirmation, and said, "So—

"Well," he said, "we heard—"

Understanding advanced over Van Horst's face, and suddenly he laughed.

"Let me tell you what you heard," he said. "You heard I had murdered my wife in dead of night and buried her body under the floor of the Corbin cabin. You heard it from Marvin. Isn't that right?"

"Well," Heimrich said.

"Well," Van Horst mimicked. "Why don't you dig it up?"

Heimrich looked a little sheepish, but said all right, they would. Meanwhile, they would like the address of the former Mrs. Van Horst.

"Just routine?" Van Horst said, cheerfully. His cheer did not encourage Heimrich, who showed it. But he stuck to it long enough to get the address, which, Van Horst warned him, was an old one.

"Well," Heimrich said, defensively, "we have to check up. A matter of routine, as you say."

Van Horst drew on his pipe and then grinned over it at Heimrich. Heimrich wavered, and nodded, and said, "All right, Mr. Van Horst." His tone was an admission. There was a pause and Weigand broke it. There were, he said, a couple of other things— But then he was interrupted by a trooper knocking at the door. Heimrich went to the door and then out into the yard with the trooper. He was gone several minutes and came back.

"You bought a new kerosene can in Brewster Friday, didn't you?" he said to Van Horst.

"Yes," Van Horst said.

"Why?"

"The old one sprang a leak. And if you want to prove that, it's on the rubbish heap behind my place. The new can is under the sink in my kitchen, full of kerosene I bought yesterday at Ireland's. Anything else you'd like to know?"

Heimrich said he guessed there wasn't, but he'd like to have a trooper look at the heap. Van Horst shrugged and said, "Why not?" indifferently, and Heimrich, after staring at him a moment, called a trooper and sent him to look. Then he motioned Weigand aside and talked to him a few moments in lowered tones. The trooper was back from Van Horst's when they finished, and nodded when Heimrich's glance questioned him.

"O.K., Lieutenant," the trooper said. "Like he says."

Heimrich nodded, and said he supposed so.

"We already knew you had bought kerosene yesterday," he told Van Horst. "The men just found out. Two gallons, wasn't it?"

"A can full," Van Horst said. "A two-gallon can full."

"You and the Fullers and Miss Corbin and the Norths, here," he said. "Your Mr. Ireland's got quite a memory. The Norths bought cream, too."

"Mr. Ireland's little joke, that is," Mr. North explained. "We've never seen what was funny about it, but it makes Mr. Ireland laugh."

"So," Heimrich said. "And nobody bought gasoline in a can; only to go in their cars, which is just about what we figured." He reflected, and asked Van Horst questions about his actions the day before. They were routine actions; none of which put Van Horst near the Corbin cabin. He seemed to have had less time than the others to leave the Fuller party, since he spent a good deal of time playing the guitar and singing. He knew nothing of why either girl should have been murdered, except—

"Well," he said, "Jean was the kind of girl who might get into trouble—play with the wrong wild animal or something. But I know of nothing definite. She just got around—and liked to keep men interested." He paused. "Not me, however," he said. "We'd had that out a long time ago."

That seemed, for the moment, to be all. Then Weigand thought of something.

"What's the kerosene can ration?" he said. "One to a house? I mean, if they go with the houses?"

They did go as part of the furnishings of the cabins, Van Horst agreed, and went one to the cabin. So far as he knew, offhand, nobody had two, but he obviously couldn't be sure. He had been in most of the kitchens and had never noticed more than one, which he supposed proved nothing in particular. Weigand thought a minute.

"Are any of the cabins vacant?" he asked.

"One," Van Horst said. "Around the lake near the dam. Marvin's cows break through over there and bother people sometimes, so it isn't popular."

"There'd be a spare can in that cabin?" Weigand said.

Van Horst said there would.

"As a matter of fact," he said, "I was over there Friday getting out one of the beds to give to the Askews, who wanted an extra, and I looked around in the kitchen to see whether there was anything worth taking over and locking up for the winter. There was a spare can there then."

"So," said Heimrich. "Well—"

"Right," Weigand said. "I think that does it, for now, anyway."

"Dismissed?" Van Horst wanted to know. Weigand nodded and smiled.

"Right," he said.

Van Horst knocked out his pipe in the fireplace, told the Norths he'd be seeing them, and went out.

"Blair?" Heimrich said. Weigand nodded.

"But first," he said, "I'd sort of like to know whether that can is still in the vacant cabin. How about sending a man around to see?"

Heimrich looked doubtful, and sent a man. Then, as he was about to send the second courier for Blair, there was a shout from the lake. They waited a moment and a trooper came up the path at a trot.

"I guess we've found it, Lieutenant!" he said. "Want to come along and see?"

They went along to see—Heimrich, Weigand and, after an inquiring exchange of glances with each other, the Norths. At the end of the lake several troopers were gathered in a knot, looking at something. They broke apart as Heimrich and his supporting cast appeared, and held up the object they had been looking at. Heimrich looked at it and said he'd be damned.

It was an ordinary grass sickle, but rather a good one, with a heavy steel blade and a long handle. It was much too good, as anyone could see, to be thrown casually in the lake, and after a glance nobody believed it had been thrown casually. Whatever may have been on it had been washed away by the water, along, Heimrich remarked, with any prints which might have been on the blade or the rough handle. But you didn't, Heimrich said, always need proof to know.

"So," he said. "That's it." He felt the point of the blade with a finger, and nodded. "Just about sharp enough," he said. "It would go in a neck easy. I guess we can figure it did go in a neck easy."

He turned it in his hands.

"Long handle," he said. "You could stand"—he held it out at arm's-length toward a trooper, who started back and then looked sheepish—"you could stand a good ways off. You wouldn't need to get blood on you. You could go back to a party and not show that anything had happened."

He turned the grass sickle in his hands, examining the handle. Then he looked at the end of the handle and said, "Huh!"

"What would 'F' stand for?" he asked.

Weigand and the Norths looked at one another.

"Well," Mr. North said, "that's obvious, of course. It could stand for Fuller. As a matter of fact, I think it is the Fullers'. And they kept it hooked over a projection in the fireplace chimney, outside the house. Where anybody could pick it up as he went past."

Heimrich nodded and said he supposed it would be that way.

Going back to the Norths' cabin, they stopped by the Fullers'. Both Jane and Ben identified the sickle readily, and said it had been kept hanging on the chimney outside the house.

"Handy for anybody at the party," Heimrich said.

Ben, the red-headed, looked at him hard and flushed.

"Sure," he said. "Absolutely. We put it there to be handy!"

"Come off it, Ben," Mr. North said. Weigand said, sure, come off it.

"After all," he said, "people have grass sickles to cut grass. Not to cut anything else. You wouldn't expect people to want to cut anything else with a sickle."

They carried the sickle back to the Norths' after Fuller had been soothed, with the help of Jane, who urged him to act his age, if he could. There was not much use examining it, after hours in the water, but you couldn't merely give it back. Heimrich turned it over to a trooper after everybody had looked at it, and discovered nothing, and the trooper put a tag on it and started an exhibit cache, against a trial when a trial came. Heimrich said, "Blair?" again and Weigand nodded and then caught himself. He suggested they might clear up some of the others, first, in case something else might crop up to give ammunition.

Then there was a quick tap at the door and a hot-looking trooper brought them more ammunition. Or brought them something—it was hard at the moment to say what. He said he had been to the unoccupied cabin.

"I oughta gone by boat," he said. "It's a helluva walk around that road."

Nobody offered sympathy. You could not count Heimrich's "Too bad" as sympathy. The trooper took a look at his superior and abandoned collateral detail.

"I went through the cabin carefully, Lieutenant," he said. "I even looked under things. There's no oilcan in that cabin." He paused. "Empty *or* full," he said, providing emphasis.

Heimrich nodded and waved him back to the yard. He looked at Weigand, inquiringly.

"Do you suppose Van Horst was lying about it?" he said. "Or—"

Weigand said he didn't think Van Horst was lying. He said he thought it was something else.

"I think the can was there Friday," he said. "I think it wasn't there yesterday. And—well, I wouldn't be surprised if it came back."

He paused a minute and shook his head thoughtfully.

"I don't like this fellow," he said. "I don't like him at all. I think he's playing tricks, and I don't like the tricks. And—I think he's been listening in on us, don't you?"

Heimrich nodded.

"And you figure he isn't done yet?" he said. He said it heavily. Weigand nodded slowly.

"I'm afraid he isn't done," he said. "I'm afraid he's collecting more ammunition—too. I think maybe we'd better hurry."

· 10 ·

But it is hard to hurry if you do not know where you are going, or even in what direction. You can hurry through questions, but not so fast that you miss the answers, and witnesses are seldom concise. The Lone Lakers who passed in review through the North living-room most of the rest of the afternoon were seldom concise, and the shadows lengthened and the setting sun began to paint the clouds, and still it seemed to the detectives, and to the Norths, that they were marking time. Pam North sat nearer Jerry as the shadows began to lengthen, and after a while her hand wandered into his, as if by accident. It had been an uneasy hand before, but it quieted in his.

The Askews came and went, and left little except an impression of utter innocence, and almost complete ignorance, behind. Mr. Hanscomb entered, conversed—he was a loquacious one—and exited, and it was clear that he had not murdered anybody and did not know who had. It was not even entirely certain that he knew anybody had been murdered. Others came from the cabins across the lake, which made up what Mrs. North said was called "drunkards' row."

"Only," she explained, "that's really from way back. Everybody who lives over there now virtually teetotals."

It took time; it took the afternoon. It was growing dusky in the cabin, although it was still light enough outside, when they sent for Thelma Smith, and while they were waiting for her to come Mr. North lighted the lamps and then, when Mrs. North suggested it, the fire. He started to pour kerosene on the logs, stopped and looked at the can oddly, and then poured the kerosene on the logs. The flames leaped up, harmlessly.

Thelma Smith's pale hair was drawn back from a long, discontented face, but her brown eyes had unexpected heat in them. She wore a white tennis dress with a green scarf at the throat which was a wrong green, and when she sat she disposed herself indifferently. She managed to convey in her tone an apparent surprise that they should find her important enough to question; there was an implication that she was commonly, and of course unjustly, overlooked.

The day before was, from her account, much as they had heard it from others. She had been met at the station Saturday morning by Kennedy and Helen Wilson. "They kept me waiting on the platform," she added. "You could always count on Wilson being late." She had lunched with the others at the Wilson house and watched the tennis for a time. Then, because it was "dull," she had wandered away, walking "down toward the lake." She had come back, however, in time to see the end of the match and "all the silly fuss people made over it." Afterward she had had dinner and gone to the party, and left it early.

"There were more women than men," she said, morosely. "There always are up here."

She had gone to bed a little while after getting back to the Wilson house and slept as well as the spare bed permitted. She was querulous about the spare bed. And all she knew about the murders was what she had heard that morning, when people got around to telling her about them.

She had no idea why anyone should mean, or do, harm to Helen Wilson. She seemed abstractedly surprised that anybody had.

"You would never expect anything to happen to her," she said.

"Anything—interesting. She always seemed a very ordinary person." She paused. "You'll think I shouldn't say that, now," she said, in a tone which indicated that she cared nothing for what they might think. Lieutenant Heimrich's face indicated clearly enough what he thought.

"Jean was different," Thelma went on, without waiting to be asked. "I should think that killing her would be a satisfaction to anyone."

There was a new, acrid note in her voice; from listlessness she seemed, as she mentioned the name, translated to something very like excitement. Bitter excitement.

"What do you mean by that?" Heimrich asked.

She wanted to know what he thought she meant. He merely waited.

"She was—*vicious*!" Thelma Smith told them. There was viciousness in her own voice as she spoke. "She was cruel and disloyal and didn't care what happened to other people as long as she got what she wanted. As long as she was all right."

"Well," said Heimrich. "So she was all right, was she?"

"Oh, *she*," Thelma Smith said. "She was always all right. I ought to know if anyone did. I took enough from her. She—"

And then it came out, rushing. Her voice was high and excited and her face flushed uglily and she leaned forward in the chair near the fire. There was no stopping the spate of words, and nobody tried to stop them. The Norths sat in the shadow close together, and Heimrich looked at her amazed, and Weigand leaned forward in his chair and looked hard at her as he listened. It was as if something had suddenly given way.

It was rather hard to follow. It dealt chiefly with the things that Jean Corbin had done, maliciously and cruelly, to Thelma Smith. Now and then, there were references to what she had done to others, but those were only references in passing—references to fill out a picture of a cold and merciless woman, grabbing from others, making others suffer out of pure malice. There were references running through it to John Blair. She had taken Blair from Thelma, it developed. It was not the first time she had done it, one gathered, although the words skirted the direct.

"Whenever she saw any man was interested in any other woman,"

Thelma told them, "she sneaked in. She knew all the tricks to fool a man, to involve him and catch him. Not that she wanted them, except to *take* them. They found that out, soon enough. I could tell you—"

She did tell them, as her narrative tumbled and circled. She brushed her pale hair back nervously, almost frantically, as she talked, and her brown eyes were hot and bitter.

Blair, it appeared, was an example. He had first been introduced to Thelma by Helen Wilson. "I was plenty good for him then," the girl said, angrily. Reticence had dropped from her as if she were talking to herself. "Oh yes, I was good enough—we got along fine." Then Jean had come in. "She saw what was going on," she said. "You could trust her for that. And you could trust her to know the tricks!"

She had used the tricks, if one could believe the story. "Things I wouldn't do. Things no decent woman would do," she told them. "He was a fool, like most men. He didn't see through her. Any woman would have seen through her. Maybe he does now!" In any case, it was clear that Jean had taken Blair, who appeared in the likeness of a disputed dummy, from Thelma. That, it developed, was the final straw—with that, Thelma ended the shared occupancy of the cabin. "She wanted me to stay, all right," she said. "You can bet she did. I was *bait*. But I'd had enough of it."

It was evident, as the story circled back again, that this was only the most recent of Jean Corbin's unbearable acts. Nor was she unbearable only in love. She was ruthless, too, in business.

"You work for the Bell firm, too, don't you?" Weigand cut in. She seemed not to hear him, although she stopped for an instant and stared at him blankly. He did not repeat the question, because it became clear in a moment that she did; that she and Jean had started with the firm together; that Jean had clawed her way to the top, or near the top.

"What did she have?" Thelma demanded. "Nothing a hundred haven't; nothing I haven't. She wasn't clever, or kind or honest. But there wasn't anything she wouldn't do—not *anything*. There wasn't anybody she wouldn't hurt, and *like* hurting. I ought to know!"

There was more of it—for a time it appeared that there would be no end of it. Piecing it together afterward, the four who heard her could reduce to some order a catalogue of Jean Corbin's unfairnesses, her ruthless cruelties. There had been, at least in Thelma's mind, a long series of stolen men, of whom Blair was the last. Now—until yesterday—she had been tiring of Blair and moving in on Dr. Abel. She had known that Mrs. Abel was aware of what she was doing, and had laughed at her. "Openly." She had gone ahead in business at the expense of others than Thelma Smith. "Everybody knows she got Hardie Saunders out," Thelma told them. "She got him out—lied about him—and got his job. Oh, she could plan things like that!" And she was never content, never generous to the defeated. "She was torturing Johnny, even when she was through with him," Thelma told them. "She didn't care what she did. She'd have got Hardie Saunders again, too."

She—she—she— It went on and on. Then it began to repeat; then the angry, shrill voice quieted and suddenly, in what seemed full course, halted. She sat and stared at Heimrich and Weigand and pushed her hair back uncertainly. Then she was on her feet.

"Oh!" she said. "Oh—why did you make me?" There was something like entreaty in her voice and a strange, fixed look in her eyes as they swept over and beyond the two detectives. Then, suddenly, she turned and, even while Heimrich was getting up to stop her, she was out of the cabin. Heimrich moved to go after her, hesitated.

"That's right," Weigand said. "Let her go. She's told us about everything."

"Well—" Mrs. North said, from the shadow of the couch. "She—she's something, isn't she," Mrs. North's voice sounded entirely incredulous. "Who'd have thought she'd do that." There was distaste, too, in Mrs. North's voice.

"She certainly hated her," Mr. North said, quietly. "It's not pretty, is it?"

Weigand said it wasn't.

"Excitement," he said. "The strain—everything. She hated her, of course. And of course there was something else."

"Something else?" Heimrich said. "What else?"

Weigand hesitated for a moment.

"Well," he said. Then, "She loved her too, of course. Didn't she?"

The question, if you could call it a question, was directed toward the Norths. There was no answer for a moment, and then Mrs. North spoke.

"Oh," she said, "yes, I suppose so. People are—well, they frighten you sometimes, don't they?"

Nobody answered and after a moment Mrs. North got up. She got up briskly, as if she were shaking free from something, and said they couldn't do anything more until they had food.

"It's after eight," she said. "And I've started nothing. Shall we try Ireland's?"

They went out, and now it was almost dark, and very quiet. It was quiet and there were deeper shadows and in one of the shadows, against the far side of the cabin, there was a shaft of darker shadow. They might have taken it for a post, if they had seen it—and if the Norths had not realized that there was, just there, nothing that was at all like a post. But nobody noticed it and the Norths and the two detectives drove down the road to Ireland's and had coffee and sandwiches. Then they came back and, avoiding for the moment any further discussion of Thelma Smith's tirade, sent the trooper named Pete to bring Hardie Saunders around. They smoked while they waited, and Mr. North, Mrs. North suggesting it, put another log on the fire. It burned up brightly, and a modified sort of cheerfulness edged back. It was not dissipated by the arrival of Hardie Saunders.

"Well," he said, standing at the door. "You look mighty comfortable in here."

There was robust sanity apparent in Mr. Saunders. He supposed they wanted to ask him some questions—about yesterday, perhaps? He was, it was clear, a cooperative witness. Heimrich guided him, starting the morning before. He and Blair had slept rather late, it developed. Then they had had breakfast, had cleaned up the cabin, filled the lamps.

"Not what *you* would call cleaning up, I suppose, Pam," he said. "Just bachelor cleaning up. No kitchen scrubbing, or anything like that. No chimney cleaning. Just a couple of males, getting along."

Mrs. North said, politely, that everything had always looked very neat when she had been in the Saunders-Blair cabin. She said she only wished she could get Jerry to fill the lamps in the morning, instead of when they ran dry, and had to be blown out.

"Leaving everything dark," she said.

Saunders agreed that that was one thing they did do. Or Blair did, rather, and always spilled kerosene on the kitchen floor. "Like yesterday, trying to get the last drops into the Aladdin," he said.

"All right," Heimrich said. "And then?"

Then, leaving a few odds and ends of waste disposal to Blair, Saunders had driven into Brewster to market. He said he wanted to be exact, however, and that wasn't quite exact. He had driven out of his way to pick up some mint over by the dam, so that they could have the last juleps of the season that afternoon, if they brought people back with them. He still had the mint, since they hadn't brought anybody back.

After he had got the mint he had driven on to Brewster and—oh, yes, had the car tank filled on the way—bought meat and vegetables for the stew, run across Kennedy and Helen Wilson shopping and said "Hello" to them, driven back to camp and found that Blair was gone. "He'd gone over to see if he could get in a set before the match, I found out afterward," Saunders told them. After Saunders put things away he went on over to the courts too, and, finding them occupied, had "strolled around" for a while and ended up at Ireland's for a bottle of beer and a sandwich, eating early so as to give digestion a chance before he played tennis. Then, when the others were ready, he and Jean had taken on the Norths.

His voice sobered as he mentioned Jean. He said it was a tragedy, all right. "She was a fine girl," he said. "She was going places." There was nothing but sadness and admiration in his voice, Weigand thought. He interrupted.

"We gathered from somewhere," he said, "that she was—well, rather ruthless in getting somewhere. Did you find her so?"

Hardie Saunders looked surprised and puzzled. He said he couldn't guess who had given them that idea unless, as an afterthought, Thelma Smith? He read the truth of that guess in Heimrich's face, and laughed without enjoyment.

"I wouldn't take what she says too seriously," he advised them. "She's—well, she collects grudges. When life isn't seamy enough, she sits down and runs herself a seam."

Weigand said that Jean Corbin hadn't, then, had anything to do with Saunders' leaving Bell, Halpern & Bell? Hardie Saunders looked surprised and shook his head. He said of course not.

"As a matter of fact," he said, "I saw a chance to pull out and take a pretty good account with me and start for myself. So I pulled. What gave you the idea Jean had anything to do with it? Thelma again?"

"Partly," Weigand said. "Chiefly, I guess. You wouldn't agree, then, that Miss Corbin was the sort of person to make a good many enemies?"

Saunders said he certainly wouldn't. That was what made it so baffling. Everybody liked her, except Thelma, of course—it was incredible that anyone at camp should want to harm her. That was why he thought it must be some person from outside. Had they thought of that?

"Yes," Heimrich said. "We've thought of that, of course. Or it may have been merely that she stumbled on something about the other murder and had to be got out of the way."

Saunders nodded, slowly, agreeingly.

"Only," he said, "if that's the case why should anybody want to kill Helen Wilson?"

"You can't think of any reason?" Heimrich asked. Hardie Saunders, big and red-faced and jovial-looking, but just now grave, couldn't think of any reason.

They led him on through the day. After tennis he had gone back to the cabin and put on the stew over a slow fire, then came to the Norths and had a drink or two, then returned to his own cabin and found Blair already there. They had had another drink or two, and then the stew and then, toward nine-thirty, gone to the party at the Fullers'. There, like everybody else, he had been in and out a couple of times, and could not remember the times. He waited inquiringly, and when there were no more questions for a moment started to rise. Then Weigand said there was one thing more; rather a personal thing.

"We've gathered," he said, "that you and Jean were—well, call it quite friendly, at one time. Right?"

Hardie Saunders looked confused and then a little resentful and said, "Now, listen—" Then he interrupted himself and smiled, a little shamefacedly. He said he supposed there were no secrets, under these circumstances.

"All right," he said. "I would have liked to be—quite friendly. She thought otherwise. No grudge, or anything. Best of friends afterward and all that." He smiled. "I could see her point," he said. "I was sort of big and blundering to her, I guess." He was very disarming, and waited for more questions with a half-smile. But there were no more questions, as it turned out. He had a few of his own. How were they getting on? Were they sure, after all, that Jean had been murdered? They were polite in answering, uninformatively. He took the implied dismissal, said he was around when they wanted him and started out.

"By the way," he said, "you aren't keeping us around tomorrow or anything like that, are you? I mean, most of us have jobs to do in town, you know. Several people have asked me, and I promised to find out."

Heimrich and Weigand consulted with their eyebrows, and Heimrich said he supposed it would be all right for most of them to go back to town, and that he would decide and let them know. Saunders looked rather disappointed, started to say something more and decided against it; went along.

"That is a point," Weigand said, after he had gone. "What do you plan to do about it? These people are all weekenders here, of course. It won't be convenient for many of them to stay around; you'd have trouble making them, if they didn't want to."

Heimrich said that, as things stood now, he was inclined to let most of them go in, provided they promised to keep themselves available in town. He said he'd see how things worked out, and that he thought they had better get on to Blair. Pete, the trooper, went after Blair.

John Blair was in his middle twenties and his voice drawled with the South. He smoothed his dark hair with his hand as he sat down, and then ran his fingers through it and ruffled it again. He moved often in his chair as he answered questions, tracing his activities the day and

night before. He had, on Saturday morning, helped Saunders straighten
the cabin; then, when Saunders went to market, he had burned waste-
paper and buried garbage. After that he had gone looking for tennis,
and got in a set before the tournament match. He had gone to Van
Horst's afterward, left early and returned to the cabin. Then, as it was
beginning to get chilly, he had built a fire and sat looking at it until
Saunders came along. He was entirely alone, and the time was about
an hour.

He smoothed his hair and upset it again.

"I was alone a good deal of yesterday," he said, worriedly. "So if
you're looking for alibis—" He had been alone for an hour and a half
between the time Saunders had left in the morning and the time he
found a tennis adversary. Between their set and the match he had
strolled around, looking for excitement, not finding it.

"Did you see anybody else strolling around?" Weigand inquired,
idly.

Blair had, although not to speak to. He had seen Dorian Hunt walking, with no particular intention evident in her walk. "Where?" Over
toward the dam; in that direction, anyway. She was too far away to
speak to.

He had been with others during the tournament match and afterward
until he had gone back to his own cabin. And after dinner he had been
with others, at the party, and had still been there when Helen Wilson's
body was found. And—

"Well, that's about all of it," he said. "I don't know whether it
means anything."

He was nervous, they thought, watching him.

"You and Jean were close—friends?" Heimrich asked.

Blair shifted in his chair. Then he nodded.

"And she was making you jealous?" There was hardly a question in
the statement. "With Dr. Abel?"

Blair sat up suddenly, and spoke quickly.

"There's no truth in that!" he said. "It's a lie people have been
telling!"

He was emphatic about it, and bitter. And yet his emphasis seemed, somehow, a little hollow. Heimrich nodded, without comment, and shifted.

"You may as well know," he said, "that we've found out about the money."

Blair echoed it. "The money?" he said. Heimrich stared at him and waited. "You mean the Brownley money?" Their faces told him that they did. He flushed quickly, and then the color left his face. He looked startled, frightened. It was clear that he followed all the implications that went with the Brownley money, and his inheritance after Helen Wilson. It was also clear that he was frightened.

He stood up and tried to make his voice firm, but the voice shook.

"You can't tie me up in it!" he said. "You're twisting things! You're trying to make it look—" He stopped, seeing no response in the faces. He stared at them.

"Listen," he said. "You can't get away with this!"

Still nobody said anything for several moments, and then Weigand spoke.

"With what?" he said. His voice was soft and inquiring, but his face was not soft. Blair stared at him and he stared back.

"Well," said Blair, "what are you going to do about it? If you think you've got something on me, what are you going to do about it?" He finally got challenge into his tone, his first excitement steadying. He was, Weigand thought, getting control of himself. Weigand suspected that, at the moment, Blair would not be saying any more.

"I don't think we'll do anything just now, Mr. Blair," Weigand said, softly. "Except—" He paused and consulted Heimrich, inquiringly. Heimrich nodded. "We'd like you to stay around, Mr. Blair," he said. "We may want to talk to you again tomorrow."

Blair looked at them, and then spoke explosively.

"Sure!" he said. "Sure I'll stick around. And you won't do anything to me, because I didn't have anything to do with it, see?"

It sounded, Weigand thought, like bluster. He nodded indifferently in reply, ignoring the challenge.

"That's all, Mr. Blair," Heimrich said, curtly, as Blair still stood staring at them. "We'll let you know when we want to talk to you again."

Blair still hesitated, as if he meant to speak again. But then he turned and went out the door, leaving Heimrich and Weigand to look at each other. Heimrich's look was satisfied, and he nodded.

"So that's Mr. Blair," he said. "Looks like we're getting places. Motive, opportunity, I'd guess temperament. So . . . "

Lieutenant Heimrich sounded pleased. Weigand thought a moment, staring at the fire, and nodded. He said it could be.

"He's afraid," Weigand said. "He's nervous and I think he could be violent. And motive, as you say. Only I wish—"

He did not finish what he wished, but continued staring into the fire. He looked worried and distraught, Mrs. North thought, watching his profile in the firelight. When he spoke it was thoughtfully, almost as if to himself.

"I don't like the setup," he said. "Blair, or anybody else, I don't like the setup." He brooded, and then leaned back with a half-laugh.

"City man in the country, probably," he said. "I keep feeling that people are too scattered out and remote from one another in the country; that there are too many shadows and too much cover." He turned toward the Norths, and he was smiling, but uneasily. "Why the devil don't you people have electricity?" he demanded. "Why don't you light things up?"

"Well," Mr. North said, "we like them this way, generally. But it's generally perfectly calm here. Calm and simple."

Weigand walked toward the rear door, leading out on the porch, and looked out into the night. Suddenly he stiffened, said, "Hey!" and pushed the screen open violently, running out. The others started up, and heard Weigand crashing through the bush. Then there was an oath and the sound of a fall, and Heimrich and North ran toward the sound, with Mrs. North a little way behind them, flashing a torch she had grabbed up from its place on one of the couch-ends. They went about a hundred feet before they found Weigand, sitting on the ground, rubbing his head and swearing. He looked at them and swore further, and then got up. He kicked a sumach stump disgustedly, and told them they could have their country.

"Come on," he said. "He's gone now. Of all the places to chase anybody! There must be a hundred things to trip over every square yard."

He explained when they were back in the cabin. He had stood at the door a moment and then, perhaps twenty feet away in the darkness, seen a cigarette glowing. As he saw the light, the person behind it apparently saw him. The cigarette arched off to the side and Weigand heard somebody running off and ran after him. Weigand thought he was gaining when he tripped and fell. He looked disgustedly at the Norths and said that they could give him pavements.

"It was somebody listening?" Mrs. North said.

Weigand nodded, slowly, and said it looked like it.

"But what did he hear?" Mrs. North said. "And who was it?"

"Well," Weigand said, "if we knew that we'd know a lot. He could have been the man we're looking for—or the woman. And he could have heard—well, anything we've heard. As he did before, outside the kitchen window. Supposing it was the same person."

Mrs. North looked at Weigand slowly, and something like fear came into her eyes.

"I wonder what he heard?" she said. "That we didn't hear. Or didn't understand." She paused. "I wonder what he'll do about it?" she said.

• 11 •

SUNDAY
10:05 P.M. TO MONDAY, 1:15 A.M.

There had been no answer to Mrs. North's question fifteen minutes later, when Heimrich and Weigand finished checking off their possibles. The question still hung in the air; seeming to float under the roof of the cabin, where the stretchers, extending from eaves to eaves, threw heavy shadows; it waited outside the cabin, in the country darkness which hemmed in their little center of light and fire. Weigand had shaken his head over it, and let it go by default.

They had checked and discarded. There were apparent outsiders, to be ignored for the time being—most of those from "drunkards' row," such apparently detached people as the Askews and Hanscomb. "The man nobody knows," Mrs. North said of Hanscomb, and proved by being unable to amplify. There were a few to be marked free from suspicion for other reasons. Mrs. Wilson. "Dorian Hunt?" Weigand said. Heimrich said, "Why?" and Weigand, after thinking a moment, nodded, and did not divulge his own reason, which was simply that he couldn't imagine her killing—and, he was surprised to discover, was definitely antagonized by the idea. The Norths.

"I think," Mr. North said, "that that's mighty white of both of you. Mighty white."

Mrs. North told him not to be silly. She said she'd like to catch Bill suspecting them. "Again," she added. Weigand looked at her and smiled, and denied he ever had, even a year before.

But it left them plenty. "Blair," Heimrich said. "Start with Blair." Motive, opportunity, character—all fitted.

Thelma Smith? There was no reason to leave her out. She had hated Jean Corbin, if Jean qualified as First Victim; she did not impress you as having compunctions which would stop her from killing the innocent in self-defense.

James Harlan Abel? "He'd kill anybody in a minute if they got in his way," Mrs. North assured them, "and anything which disturbed him would be getting in his way." Perhaps Jean Corbin had been bothering him and he had brushed her aside. It seemed insufficient. "But not for him, maybe," Mrs. North insisted.

Mrs. Abel? Jealousy would cover her, if it were true that Jean had been trying to entice her husband. She was neurotic, they agreed.

The Fullers? It was their sickle, but that was for them rather than against them. No motive was apparent. "Count them out?" Weigand inquired; and Heimrich, after a moment's hesitation, nodded. "Of course!" said Mrs. North, with some indignation. "Just like us." She did not amplify, and Heimrich looked faintly puzzled, but went on.

Hardie Saunders? There was opportunity—there seemed to be opportunity for almost everyone, particularly with the time of one crime vague and the positions of no one at the time of the other assured, or assurable. His character was against murder, apparently. His motives, if they existed, were indecisive.

Van Horst? Unless one believed old Marvin, there was no motive. And it was hard to believe old Marvin.

"How about Marvin himself?" Heimrich said. "If we're looking further than Blair, that is. I've always thought he was dangerous, and he's crazy enough not to need a motive. Maybe he just doesn't like women to wear pants."

"Well," said Mrs. North, "he'd have to be crazy. He wears pants, doesn't he?"

"Barely," Mr. North assured her.

Heimrich smiled, but said he was serious—half-serious, anyway. They had to leave Marvin in as a possible. You could never tell what strange grudge he might hold against either girl.

Arthur Kennedy? Why? "Well," Weigand said, "there might be a connection. He's in the street; Helen Wilson used to be in the street. And Dorian's father—" He stopped, and looked worried.

"I guess we can't leave her out," he admitted, and Mrs. North heard regret in his tone and looked at him speculatively, and then smiled a little to herself. "She may have blamed Helen for her father's trouble. I don't think it's likely, but it's a motive."

Heimrich nodded. He said he thought Weigand would have to come back to that. He added, however, that he still favored Blair.

"I'm tempted to pick him up," he said, thoughtfully. "Maybe we could persuade him to talk. Only—"

"Right," Weigand said. " 'Only.' I think I wouldn't yet anyway. You've no evidence for the D.A. It—"

Since they had returned to the cabin after Weigand's abortive pursuit of the eavesdropper, the New York detective had been sitting where he could look out the door that gave onto the porch. Now, staring abstractedly across the lake, he broke off and got up and went to the door. He beckoned with a flip of his hand and the others joined him, Mrs. North on tiptoe to see over Weigand's shoulder.

"What?" she said. "I don't see anything."

Her voice was low, almost a whisper. Weigand pointed.

"Over there," he said. "It looked like a flashlight. There!"

They all saw it—a sudden point of light. It went out as they watched.

"Where would that be?" Weigand demanded, hurriedly.

"The dam camp," Mr. North told him. "It's empty, but somebody's fooling around."

"Right!" said Weigand. "Somebody's fooling around." He turned to

Heimrich. "I'm tired of people fooling around," he said. "We'll fool around a bit ourselves."

Heimrich nodded.

"Car," he said. "Does the road run that far?"

Mr. North nodded. You could get within a hundred yards of the camp by the back road which, winding halfway around the lake, went on beyond it and later joined the main road from Route 22 to Patterson.

"Come on!" Weigand said. "We'll take my car."

The two detectives crossed the living-room, moving fast. Mr. North started to follow them, but when he reached the door he stopped. He turned back, and hesitated. He looked at Mrs. North.

"Boat," he said. "Whoever it is could cross back by boat while they were going around. I ought to have told them."

Mrs. North nodded.

"So," said Mr. North, "I've got to cut across by boat myself, to cover that. You stay here." He started for the door, but Mrs. North caught his arm. She said he wasn't going to do anything of the kind.

"Listen," Mrs. North said. "You don't understand! He's a murderer. He kills people. If you think I'm going to let you—"

"I'll be all right, Pam," Mr. North told her, breaking in. "I'll be careful."

"—go alone," Mrs. North finished, "you're crazy, Jerry. If anybody's going to kill you, I'm going to be there."

She stopped and listened to herself. She said that that sounded funny. "Anomalous," she said. "I mean they'll have to kill me, too. Come on."

Mr. North wanted to argue further, but it is hard to argue with a wife who is running down a dark path, with only a little moonlight to guide her, toward a boat landing. Mr. North caught up a flashlight and ran after her, and remembered not to yell. He caught her at the landing and started to argue, but she climbed into the boat and untied the painter, and seemed about to go on without him. He made the stern seat, crept past her cautiously, and took the oars. He started to say something, but Mrs. North said, "Right oar, hard," and by the time he had obeyed they were, somehow, irretrievably on their way over dark water from which mist was rising. Mr. North had, he realized, forgotten about the mist. But he went on, and Mrs. North guided him. They were less than half-way across when they saw the lights of a car on the far shore, swinging in toward the dam camp. The lights stopped and the smaller light of a flash moved dimly, through the gathering mist, toward the cabin.

"Bill and Lieutenant Heimrich," Mrs. North said. "Listen!" They listened, and heard nothing. "I thought maybe yells," Mrs. North said. "Or shooting. Maybe he's got away."

"And maybe," Mr. North pointed out, "he's coming our way. Keep your voice down."

"I think we should have thought," Mrs. North said. "Why wouldn't he just run down the other side? Why use a boat?"

There was, Mr. North realized, no reason at all why whoever it was, assuming it was somebody with guilty intentions, should not retreat along the shore opposite the Norths' cabin. That gave him another idea.

"We'll cut straight across," he said. "Head him off!"

He veered the boat away from the dam end of the lake, and leaned on the oars for the opposite side. The lake was narrow; even with Mr. North's rowing it took only a little time to cross. The boat went aground in mud, however, while a couple of feet still separated it from the far bank. Mrs. North started to move, but Mr. North caught her arm and pulled her back.

"I'll jump," he said. "You wait in the boat—sit as far back as you can, to lift the front end. Then I can pull it up." He spoke in a whisper, and Mrs. North nodded. Mr. North inched his way to the prow, and leaped across to a sodden shore. He found firmer ground, grabbed the painter and began to pull. Then a noise made him whirl, dropping the line.

There was a disturbance in the brush off to his right, and Mr. North ran toward it. It was a floundering noise as of some heavy, squirming thing, and as Mr. North rushed toward it it stopped. Only then did he remember the flashlight he had thrust into his pocket. He dragged it out and aimed its beam ahead. There was nothing to be seen in the dim radiance it painted on the mist. He went on, making better time, although there was no path. He heard Mrs. North call after him, softly: "Jerry! Jerry!"

"Yes," he called, since there was no point in trying to hide his presence. "Yes. In a minute! There's—"

Then his voice was cut off and he was staring at the ground. There was a figure lying doubled up at his feet, and Mr. North dropped to his knees beside it.

"It's a man, this time," Mr. North was thinking, with horror in his thoughts, even as he turned the face upward and identified the man. It was John Blair. And then there was movement behind Mr. North and, by instinct, he flung up an arm. There was sharp pain in the arm, and it dropped. Then a sudden flash spread through Mr. North's world, and blackness blotted it, and Mr. North had time for only one more thought before the blackness swept over him.

"Well," Mr. North thought, absurdly, but with a kind of triumph at his perspicacity. "So he hadn't gone away, after all!"

It was Mr. North's belief, when he learned later what had happened, that Pam had saved his life, and this conviction he did not afterward abandon. Pam North, after it was all over, said that she, at any rate, agreed with him and added that it was a comfort, finally, to find him appreciating her. But Weigand was never much convinced by their theory. Mr. North's assailant, Weigand thought, had merely hit Mr. North and run at once and would not in any circumstances have waited to strike again.

"He wasn't trying to kill you," Weigand pointed out to Mr. North that same night, as Mr. North reclined uncomfortably on the couch in the cabin, his head securely bound up and his right arm in a sling. "You didn't know anything."

Mr. North felt that this was a too sweeping way to phrase it and said so, but Bill Weigand brushed his protest aside, having more serious things to think of.

"You were in the way," Weigand reasoned. "You might chase and identify. So it was handiest to knock you out. It didn't matter much to him, of course, whether you came out of it or not, so long as you didn't come out of it too quick. Even if Pam hadn't gone charging in, you'd be just about where you are now."

Mr. North's head ached and he didn't argue, but he still thought Pam had saved his life. He shivered a little to think of it, because there was, after all, no assurance that the assailant had gone. He had heard Mrs. North call; he might very well have been waiting for her to come.

She had, it became clear afterward, gone fast. When Mr. North stopped speaking in mid-sentence she had tensed, and waited a minute, and while she was waiting she had heard sounds of movement from the brush near where she guessed he had been. Then she moved. She stumbled and fell getting out of the boat, and hardly knew it; she pulled herself out of the mud and ran, calling, "Jerry! Jerry!" It was only a moment before she found him, and found that he was breathing. She saw that there was someone else lying near him, but the other person was nobody of hers, and she was holding Jerry's head in her lap and calling as loudly as she could call for help when he opened his eyes. He opened his eyes and blinked and said, "Hello, kid." But he remembered nothing of that afterward.

Weigand and Heimrich were leaving the vacant cabin and about to reenter their car when they heard Mrs. North's cries, and it took them a little time to reach her. They might have gone on foot down the path on that side of the lake, but it was strange territory to both, and they wasted time by driving back to the Norths' cabin in the car. They wasted as little time as they could and stay anywhere near the rough road, but they wasted some. And they wasted more rowing across the lake after they found a second boat. So it was between ten and fifteen minutes before they reached the Norths, and then Mr. North was fully conscious, although not up to much. He was sitting rather dizzily, with his back against a little tree and his right arm dangling uselessly, and insisting that Mrs. North see whether there was anything to do for Blair. Because Blair, too, was still alive. He was breathing heavily and when Weigand found the pulse it was weak and reedy, but Blair was alive.

Weigand stayed with the Norths, and propped Blair's head on a coat while Heimrich rowed back across the lake, churning wildly in the dark water and almost losing his way in the still thickening mist, and started things going. Then, for the third time in less than twenty-four hours, an ambulance hurried to Lone Lake, its siren commanding right of way, and an interne from the Brewster Hospital examined both victims. Mr. North's head was only bumped, but his arm was broken. But the interne shook his head over Blair, talked of fracture and concussion, and looked worried. There was room in the ambulance for Blair and North and, because she insisted so anxiously, Mrs. North too. Weigand went behind in his car to bring them back.

The Norths and Weigand came back in a reasonably short time. Mr. North's arm was set and if his face was, for a while, almost as white as the bandages, there was nothing to worry about.

"A nice, clean break," the house surgeon told him, approvingly, and Mr. North felt as if he should be proud. The bump on the head—partly, no doubt, because of the protecting arm—was nothing more than a bump, hardly worth binding up. But the scalp was nicked and the surgeon conscientious, so that Mr. North looked—and pretty much felt—a dire casualty.

There was nothing "nice," even to the surgeon, in Blair's injuries. He had been hit hard, and with intent, and his skull was fractured. Prognosis was difficult; an X-ray would tell them more. Meanwhile he was unconscious and apt to remain so for many hours, even if he did, eventually, regain consciousness. That was by no means certain.

"I'll tell you what *is* true," Weigand said, when they were back at the cabin and were discussing Mrs. North's intervention. "Whatever saved your life, you saved his, Jerry. If he lives. Because the attack on Blair is pretty clearly unfinished business."

"But why?" Mrs. North said. "I thought you thought it *was* Blair. I mean, that he was the man. So why would the murderer upset that by hitting him? Why wouldn't the murderer think it was just dandy for you to suspect Blair, and wait and see what you did about it?"

Weigand shook his head, and said they didn't know enough to answer that. There were too many chances; too much uncertainty. How, for example, could the real murderer know that they suspected Blair?

Wasn't it, even, mere speculation to assume that Blair had been hit by the murderer?

They raised their eyebrows at that. Weigand nodded. It was improbable, on the face of it, but Blair might still be their man. And his assailant? Well, what would they think of the theory that the person who hit Blair had been, not the murderer, but someone out to get the murderer, and get him without waiting for the law?

They looked as if they would not think much of it.

"Right," said Weigand. "Neither do I, as a matter of fact. But it's possible. Suppose somebody like, say Thelma Smith—all tangled up emotionally; hating Jean Corbin and loving her at the same time—discovered that Blair had really killed Jean. What would she do? I don't know. Do you?"

The Norths thought a moment, and then Mr. North shook his head, immediately wishing he hadn't. It hurt. But it was true that he didn't know what Thelma would do. Neither, it appeared, did Mrs. North. "Only not hit people," she thought, and Weigand nodded agreement to that. "Unless she went sort of crazy, as she might," Mrs. North added. Weigand nodded agreement to that, too.

And if Blair were not the murderer, there were several possibilities. For one thing, somebody had been eavesdropping through much of the questioning, and something that Blair said might have frightened the eavesdropper, who was probably the murderer. Somehow, say, Blair revealed that he knew something dangerous, and so had to be got out of the way.

"What?" said Mrs. North. "What did Blair say, if what he said gave something away? Did you hear it?"

Weigand had already been thinking of that, and had to shake his head.

"No," he said. "If it was that way, we've missed something. I don't know what. And if the murderer did hear anything of what Blair said, he probably heard enough to realize that Blair was building up a case against Blair, not against anybody else."

He looked at them and they looked at him. He smiled a little, not happily.

"Confusing, isn't it?" he said. "A policeman's life."

"What we need," Mrs. North said, "is coffee. I'll make it, only talk loud so I can hear."

"Well," said Weigand, pitching his voice so that Mrs. North could hear him in the kitchen, "here's another possibility. Blair had some reason to suspect the murderer, and knew it himself—I mean, it wasn't just a fact of which he didn't realize the significance; it was something he understood, and which pointed clearly at the murderer. So—"

"Where *is* Lieutenant Heimrich?" Mrs. North said from the kitchen. Weigand said that Heimrich was checking up on things.

"He'll be back," Weigand added. "Where was I?"

"So—" Mrs. North echoed, from the kitchen. "What Blair knew."

Weigand said, "Oh.

"Well," he said, "suppose Blair had a hunch who the murderer was and then, going away from here, perhaps, saw something that made him suspicious and followed along to investigate. And suppose the murderer heard him, or saw him, and laid what we might call an ambush and, when Blair stumbled into it, slugged him."

"I like that theory best," Mrs. North said, making rattling sounds with the coffee-pot. "Only what was the murderer doing that was suspicious? Have you any idea about that?"

She came in and sat down and said she had to wait for the kettle to boil. She looked quickly at Mr. North, who was lying back on the pillows with his eyes closed. But his color was all right, and as she watched he opened his eyes, intercepted her gaze and smiled. Mrs. North smiled back.

"Well," Weigand said, patiently. "Do you two want to listen?" She looked at him quickly, and he was smiling at them. There was a friendly sympathy and understanding in his smile.

Mr. North opened his eyes and Mrs. North turned to Weigand.

"*Have* you any idea *what* the murderer was doing, if Blair was following him and saw?" she said.

Weigand nodded.

"As a matter of fact," he said, "we have. A very good idea. Have you two forgotten what started this? The light in the empty cabin?"

"No," Mr. North said. "I was going to ask—did you find something there?"

"Yes," Weigand said. "We found something there, all right."

"Somebody murdered?" Mrs. North asked. Her voice sounded shocked. Weigand smiled.

"Not this time," he said. "Although I know how you feel. No; we found a can—just a can."

"A can?" Mrs. North said.

"A two-gallon can, made to hold kerosene," Weigand explained. "There wasn't any kerosene in it. It was the can that wasn't there this afternoon. Somebody put it back."

"Oh!" said Mrs. North.

"Right," Weigand said. "Somebody used it, as we thought, and tonight he put it back. Wiped it off very nicely too, I suspect. That's one of the things Heimrich is checking up on."

"But why?" Mrs. North said.

That, Weigand pointed out, was easy. They couldn't be allowed to find the extra can the murderer had needed, to change gasoline for kerosene at the Corbin cabin, in the murderer's possession. The simplest thing was to put the can back where he got it. So he did.

"Tidying up," Weigand said. "They do sometimes." He paused. "And sometimes that's the very way they give themselves away."

"Did he?" Mrs. North said. "This one, I mean?"

Weigand shook his head.

"No," he said. "Not that I can see at the moment. But maybe he'll get too tidy, as time goes on."

There was a rap at the door, and Heimrich followed it in. He inquired after Mr. North and said he certainly looked banged up. He had just telephoned the hospital and asked after Blair. There was no change, and as yet no certainty. Blair might live and he might not. He had learned from Van Horst that the can discovered in the empty cabin was, as nearly as Van Horst could remember, the can which was supposed to be there. He had also learned that there were no prints on the can, but merely a glove smudge on the handle. The smudge of an ordinary cotton work-glove, apparently.

Weigand nodded and said he had expected that, naturally. "Naturally," Heimrich nodded.

"Well," Weigand said, "where was everybody? Or where did everybody say?"

Heimrich looked annoyed, and said that that had turned out to be something. He said you'd think people would stay home nights, but apparently nobody had. Weigand looked sympathetic, and waited.

Heimrich, dividing the round with Sergeant Kelty, his second in command, had tried to check on the whereabouts of all the cabin occupants at the time of the attack on Blair and Mr. North. They had found it heavy going.

"Take the Wilson house," he said. "Somebody persuaded Mrs. Wilson to take a sedative right after dinner and she went to her room and went to sleep. Apparently she's still asleep. And Thelma Smith went to her room after she fixed the dinner for the two of them and had washed up. She could have gone out and come back half a dozen times with nobody the wiser, however."

Art Kennedy and Dorian Hunt weren't there at all, after about six. They decided it would be easier for Mrs. Wilson if they got away for a while, so they drove into Brewster in Kennedy's car for dinner.

"Anyway, that's what the Smith girl says," Heimrich added. "They're not back yet; must be quite a dinner."

"Right," Weigand said. "They're together, anyway."

His voice sounded cold, and his mind felt rather cold. It let Dorian out of it, clearly; except for remotely probable collaboration between her and Kennedy. But it also put her with Kennedy. Weigand was surprised to find himself not liking Kennedy. He kept thinking of a phrase he was sure he had never used, and did not think he had ever heard, and applying it to Kennedy. "Unlicked cub," Weigand said to himself about Kennedy, with animus.

"Of course," Heimrich said, "there's no way of knowing they've been together all this time. They could have come back and separated when they got here for some reason and—"

"Right," Weigand said. "That's clear enough. How about the rest?"

Heimrich looked faintly surprised at the irascibility in Weigand's tone. He told about the rest.

Dr. Abel had, according to his own account, run out of cigarettes about—

"What time did this happen?" Mr. North said. "Did anybody notice?"

It had happened, Weigand told him, a few minutes after eleven o'clock—say 11:10. It was almost one o'clock now.

Dr. Abel, Heimrich went on, had run out of cigarettes a little before eleven, and, thinking he wanted some exercise anyway, walked the mile or so from his cabin to Ireland's and then walked back. He had stayed at Ireland's a while, so it had taken him at least three-quarters of an hour. During that time, Mrs. Abel had been alone in the cabin.

The Fullers had, at any rate, stayed at home, according to their joint account. Nobody had come in.

Hardie Saunders, after leaving the North cabin and the detectives, had walked along the path to his own cabin, according to his own statement. Blair had been there, then, but a trooper came after him in a few minutes. Saunders had sat around in front of the fire, by himself and having a drink, and waited for Blair to come in. Blair hadn't come.

Van Horst had had dinner with the Askews, stayed until about eleven and then walked home. He said he had got home by ten after eleven, but nobody had seen him. Old Marvin had, his daughter had told them with considerable asperity, gone to Danbury with some friends, and might be expected to come home, drunk, any time in the next few hours. "Or few days," she added, disgustedly.

Several of the occupants of the cabins in "drunkards' row," which was some distance up from the shore on the far side of the lake, had gathered in one of the cabins and discussed various things, including the murders, and any one of them might have gone out and—

"I think," Weigand said, "that our man or woman—either could have done any of the things that have been done—is somewhere in the group we've been concentrating on. If he isn't, God help us." He paused. "We could do with His help anyway," he added. "Failing that, I think I'll go to New York tomorrow—today."

"What's that?" Heimrich said, suspiciously. "I thought we'd agreed that you—"

Weigand held up a hand to stop him and advised him to take it easy.

"I'm sticking around," he said. "I'll be back in the evening. But I have a hunch there's a city end to this thing that we don't know enough about. There's something in the past of all these people, and it's a city past. This is only where they play, remember. The city's where they work."

Heimrich began to nod agreement as the other spoke.

"Where they work," he said. "And where they get into trouble, maybe. So—"

· 12 ·

MONDAY
9 A.M. TO 11:40 A.M.

Lone Lake and the cabins scattered around it looked calm and peaceful enough at nine—no, nine-five—in the morning. The sun slanted across green grass, and trees still green as with midsummer threw long shadows. But even the shadows were bright. The lake itself was quiet and shining under the sun, and only the most modest of ripples moved across in procession, treading on one another's heels. It did not look to be a place of murder; did not, anyway, until you caught through the trees a glimpse of the charred front wall and partly fallen roof of the Corbin cabin, or until you saw the police motorcycles leaning on their standards in front of Ireland's store.

There weren't, Weigand thought as he turned by the store and went back along the road he had first traversed some forty-odd hours before, nearly enough cops. The interdict to movement which he and Heimrich had finally decided upon when they called Sunday a day after it was by more than an hour Monday, would take some enforcing. Anybody who wanted to ignore it, and go to a little trouble, could leave the lake almost at will and go to New York or where he chose. Anybody who wanted to leave could go a long way, if he chose, and leave them to chase after. A cordon around a hundred acres, wooded and undergrown, with paths in all directions and roads in most, would have, Weigand decided, to be quite a cordon. But perhaps moral suasion would suffice; certainly one might assume it would suffice to keep at the lake all who had nothing in particular on the conscience, or no great compulsion to go elsewhere. The trouble was that that group would probably not include a murderer.

"Not that it wouldn't be a help if somebody did decide to run for it," Weigand told himself, as he turned into Route 22 and headed for New York. The speedometer needle of the Buick climbed contentedly around the dial. It hesitated at fifty, while Weigand thought abstractedly; it was encouraged by his returned attention and went around to sixty. It revolved to sixty-five and then to seventy as the car rolled downgrade and swung on a broad curve. It subsided abruptly as Weigand braked for a hidden roadside and circled back when the hidden road was empty. Then it sagged back again as the car slowed for the curve into Brewster, ignored the by-pass road, and poked into town. Weigand parked neatly within the diagonal markings to the curb and went for a telephone. There were papers spread on a shelf before a store and he picked one up, dropping pennies.

The Lone Lake murders would do better if there weren't a war, he thought, but they were doing rather well. Left-hand side of the page instead of right, of course, but two columns in the *Herald Tribune* and a deep single column head in the *Times* and the whole of the first column. Breaking too late Saturday for the Sunday mornings, the story had lain dormant over Sunday and been worked on thoroughly. Running quickly down the *Times* column, Weigand saw that they had most of it, and some background. They had identified Dorian Hunt as the daughter of Clayton Hunt, for one thing. And Helen Wilson was placed as Hunt's former secretary, who had testified at his trial. The *Times* writer had been inclined to favor Helen Wilson as what one might call the pivotal victim, apparently. There was less about Jean Corbin.

"I should have been quicker with this call," Weigand thought, as he headed for a drugstore with a public telephone shield in its window. He made for the two booths in the rear.

The door of one of the booths was closed and there was a presence within it, vague to Weigand's abstraction. The other booth was empty, and Weigand pulled its door closed behind him. Gasping slightly, he reopened it partly. The previous occupant had, apparently, spent a long time in it, smoking a cigar of particular violence. Weigand fished in his pocket for a coin and lifted the receiver from the hook. Then he halted, with the receiver held in air, and listened. The door of the next booth must also be a crack open, or the soundproofing was markedly inadequate. At any rate, what the person next door was saying was almost clear.

It was a man, and some familiarity in the voice caught Weigand's mind. He could not instantly place it, but he could listen. That was a cop's prerogative.

"—that's all," the voice said, in a tone of direction. "If they ask you anything, you never heard of her. Or—make it you have heard of her, just; you have an uncertain feeling that she was somebody I knew slightly. Do you understand?" There was a pause. "What?" the man said, and then, after another pause: "Of course not. That is why there is no reason for me to be involved, or embarrassed." There was another interval for speech at the other end. "No," the man's voice said, "not today. Yes, cancel that. I can't even guess how long." There was still another pause. "Quite," the voice said. "That is precisely what I mean. I shall rely on you, then."

There was a click as the receiver went up. The door scraped and a tall man came out—a tall, lean man, with an air of very superior confidence, and just a touch of academic abstraction. Weigand said, "Well!" to himself as Dr. James Harlan Abel crossed the drugstore and exited with dignity.

So there was somebody Dr. Abel wished for the moment, not to be known as knowing, was there? Or should it be "of having known"? Weigand thought of following and finding out and decided it would keep. He looked up a number and gave it to the operator. He got back his nickel and deposited forty cents. A sweet impersonal voice told him it was Bell, Halpern & Bell good-morning. Weigand wanted to speak to somebody in charge, and gave his name.

"Lieutenant William Weigand," he added, for emphasis. "Of the Homicide Bureau."

It got results. It got the second Bell, no less. The second Bell spluttered. He was an excited Bell, full of grievance, and with, it developed, his hair full of newspaper reporters. Weigand told him, crisply, what was wanted. Nobody, insider or outsider, was to be allowed to disturb anything in Jean Corbin's office. Or in Helen Wilson's or, further, in Thelma Smith's. The second Bell said, "Quite," and that he understood, to the first two. He said, "But, Lieutenant—" to the last.

"Miss Smith is no longer with us," the second Bell explained. "Friday was her last day. I've no doubt that she cleared out her desk before she left, and we moved Miss Collins up to her desk this morning."

"Fired?" Weigand inquired, with rude directness.

The second Bell did not approve the word. But from his circumlocution it developed that the word would, rather crudely of course, fit the fact. Miss Smith had, to put it more delicately, resigned. Her resignation had, to be sure, been requested. Weigand said, "Um-m-m," thinking it over.

"I'm driving in now," he said. "I'd like to talk to you when I arrive. Will you see that it's possible?"

The second Bell indicated that he was a very busy man, of course, but that it would be made possible. Weigand left the telephone booth with a couple of new things to think over. A steaming globe of coffee beckoned him from the soda-counter, and he responded gratefully. He drank coffee and thought it over. Then a third thing to think over appeared. It appeared in a gray-green woolen dress that had come from some place where dresses were ably contrived, and a gray-green hat of barely darker shade with a jaunty ornament of yellow. It moved with unmistakable lightness and grace in clicking brown shoes, that looked at once sturdy for the country and impracticable for art. Watching Dorian Hunt pass him unseeing and walk toward the evidently very popular telephone booths in the rear, Bill Weigand decided that she dressed for town precisely as he had hoped she would dress. Lieutenant Weigand wondered what the hell she was up to, and why she had ignored the explicit instruction to remain at camp. He decided to find out.

Her telephone call was brief. She came from the booth toward him and this time he stood up, waiting. There was an almost imperceptible break in the rhythm of her walk as she saw him, but then she came on. She acknowledged his presence, and their previous contact, with a movement of the head which was as noncommittal as it might be, and was about to pass on.

"No, Miss Hunt," Weigand said. "I'm afraid you'll really have to see me. Or had you forgotten you are supposed to be at the lake?"

She stopped and turned toward him.

"All right, Lieutenant," she said. "It's necessary for me to go to town. So I decided to go to town. I'm catching the 9:40. And if you and Lieutenant Heimwahr object, I'm very sorry."

"Heimrich," Weigand explained. "As no doubt you remembered perfectly. Why is it necessary for you to go to town?"

She considered the question and decided to answer it. But her tone made it clear that the answer was purely voluntary.

"I have some sketches to deliver," she said. "To Braithwaite's. They are due this morning, and I deliver sketches when they are due. Making sketches is, you see, the way I make my living. Just as you make yours hounding people."

Her voice was entirely dispassionate, which didn't help. Weigand found that he felt angry with her, which was odd. There was no reason that an uninformed slur on his occupation should stick instead of rolling off.

"I'd like to see the sketches," he said. "It would be interesting to see sketches that are more important than murder."

He held out his hand, gesturing toward the wide leather briefcase which dangled from one gray-green shoulder. When she stared at him he merely stared back, and waited. Then she said, "All right, why not?" suddenly and opened the case flat on one of the fountain stools. There were half a dozen sketches in it.

"These are the sketches," she said, lifting two from the top. "They are what is called fashion sketches, to be reproduced in newspaper advertisements." She explained slowly and carefully, obviously to the subnormal. "On this side of the sketch are some of the dresses Braithwaite's has for sale. On this side are the old-fashioned dresses which suggested them. They'll call it something like 'Today and Yesterday' probably." She looked at him, pretending anxiety. "Is it quite clear now, Lieutenant Weigand?" she asked.

He had flushed a little at her manner, but now he was entirely calm.

"Quite clear," he said. "Thank you."

"And you see they haven't anything to do with the murders, don't you?" she said. "They are just innocent drawings of tall women in dresses."

"Yes, I see," Weigand agreed. "How did you get out? The troopers were supposed to stop you."

Nobody, she said, had tried to stop her. Arthur Kennedy had explained to one of the troopers that he had to drive into Brewster for provisions, and she had simply got in the car and come along.

"On the floor, I suppose?" Weigand said, very politely.

She looked at him, and something like a smile appeared.

"Well," she said, "I found that a shoe-lace was untied when we happened to be passing the troopers and I sort of bent over."

Weigand said, "Oh," and looked at her shoes. The shoes were quite innocent of laces. Her glance followed his and remained undisturbed.

"I have quite a bit of trouble with them," she assured him. "You can see that I might?"

They would, Weigand agreed gravely, be a nuisance. There was half a smile in his eyes, and in hers; if not a smile, an abatement of distance. Weigand said that she made his course rather difficult.

"I could take you back to the lake, of course," he pointed out. "My authority runs that far, if you were doubting it. But I have other things to do, and I don't suppose you'd stay."

Her expression was clearly that of a person who would not stay. She waited, expectantly.

"Or," Weigand said, "I can leave you alone to catch your train, of course."

"Yes," Dorian Hunt said, "you can do that, can't you?"

"Or," Weigand went on, "I can drive you in, since I'm going anyway, and at least keep an eye on you for a time." He looked at her speculatively. "That might be best," he agreed with himself. "Come on."

"Are you," Dorian wanted to know, "telling me or asking me, Lieutenant Weigand?"

Weigand thought it over.

"Oh," he said, "asking. I'll get you in quicker, if that matters."

He waited her reply, he discovered, with unexpected interest.

"Well," she said, "not unless we start."

She tied up the drawings and waited while Weigand tossed coins on the fountain counter. She went, he was interested to notice, at once to his car, parked a little way down the street. Her assurance revealed a couple of things—she had identified his car at camp, she had noticed it before she entered the drugstore. Wondering a little what that meant, he held the door open for her, walked to the driver's seat, slid the car backward into traffic and forward along Main Street, turning around the traffic stanchion in front of the station. They were rolling downhill, picking up speed, when she spoke.

"Well," she said, "are you finding out things?"

He looked at her. She was looking ahead, presenting an attractive profile. He looked ahead and forked onto Route 22, picking up speed. He said that, oh yes, he was finding out things.

"Too many things," he added, abstractedly. "That you knew which car was mine, for example."

She turned and looked at him, and he could feel her looking. But he kept his eyes soberly on the curve ahead.

"Oh," she said, "I notice things. That's all."

He let the remark drop between them, dispassionately. They rolled on, picking up speed. They covered some miles in silence. Then Dorian Hunt mentioned, politely, that he drove fast and he said absently that he was in a hurry. He wondered whether he had been maneuvered, and if he had, why? And at the same time it was, he decided, pleasant to have her beside him, for whatever reason of her own.

"Do you like being a policeman?" she asked, suddenly. "I should think a man would rather sweep streets."

The tone was sharp, but it was at the same time rather puzzled. With the road straight ahead, Weigand could turn his head to look at her.

She, too, had turned—she was looking at him in what appeared to be a kind of perplexity.

"What's the matter?" he said. "Doesn't it fit?"

He was surprised that she flushed, just perceptibly.

"Oh," she said, "I hadn't thought, particularly. Don't you fit?"

Weigand, his eyes back on the road, nodded.

"Yes," he said, "I fit—the facts, anyway. Not your ideas, perhaps. And I don't mind being a policeman."

"Well, if you must know," she said, "that's what I don't understand. I should think you would—I should think anybody would. I should think that hounding people, trying to trick them, trying to catch them out and hurt them—I should think nobody would want to do that." Her voice was bitter, now; although she was quiet, she was the Dorian Hunt who had flared so angrily when the cat stood before all of them, with his captured, dangling rabbit.

"Watch the curve!" she said quickly. Weigand, who had, he guiltily realized, not been watching the curve, braked sharply. He was embarrassed, and a little annoyed.

There was a longish pause. It took them more miles on a hilly, turning road. The speedometer needle hesitated at sixty and climbed to sixty-five. They went over a crest at close to seventy, and held it. There was something savage in their movement, but Weigand was unconscious of it. Weigand believed that he was thinking, quite calmly. They were twisting toward Pines Bridge along a sharply winding road by the reservoirs before he spoke. Then he said that her attitude was, as she must know, quite unreasonable.

"There is no point in arguing it," he said, using unconsciously the phrase which is the inevitable precursor of argument; feeling conscious, more than of anything else—more than of the car, which responded mechanically to movements which he made in forgetfulness; more than of the road—of the slender young woman sitting so easily beside him. Her body seemed, he thought, to trim itself to the movement of the car as when she walked it trimmed itself to its own motion. She was looking ahead when, as he talked, he lifted his eyes now and then from the road to look at her. But he felt that, at times, she was looking at him; that her gaze swerved always only an instant before his turned to her.

They were riding now, he told her, with no more danger than it was his responsibility to guard against, because there were policemen around them. She thought of individual policemen, but it was not a question of individual policemen. That now she was, to be sure, dependent for safety against the only dangers threatening—"like the curve back there," he admitted—on one man who happened to be a policeman was beside the point. But that no molestation threatened them from without was because of a kind of abstract policemen, of police. Here, in the country; in the city, where they were going. That she could walk through New York, through men of all kinds and all impulses, and walk with no great danger, was because of the police. It was hard to visualize, unless you happened to be a policeman. You thought of traffic policemen, sometimes abusive and bullying—

"And sometimes very pleasant," she interjected, unexpectedly. "I see traffic policemen."

"Then," he told her, "you see all policemen. They keep things running in safe paths. They prevent head-on conflicts of interest. They maintain a pattern of order and, in peaceful times, it is maintained well enough so that we do not suspect that order is not any more natural than disorder."

"'And I, my lords, embody the law,' " she said. But her voice was gentler than it had been.

"Yes," he said. "You can make anything sound silly, pretentious. But I—lieutenant of detectives, no brighter than the next, no more honest, God knows no stronger or anything—I embody the law. I do, and the rookie just out of police school, and the commissioner, just as the magistrate who fines a street-walker and the justice who sits in the Supreme Court—we all embody the law. And we aren't, I grant you, always up to it. We haven't the temperaments for it, or the minds, or the honesty; we get excited and shoot when we shouldn't. We're given guns and clubs and authority, and we're no safer with such things than other men. As individuals, that is. But we embody the law; we embody order and direction, and a compulsion against violence. We make it possible—"

"Curve!" the girl said. There was an undercurrent of merriment in her voice.

Weigand braked and said, "Damn!" and then, because there was no curve to speak of, laughed.

"Well," she said, "there could have been, for all you knew. You're a funny sort of policeman, aren't you?"

She was looking at him, now, and smiling quietly. He felt rather absurd, but also obscurely contented.

"Right," he said. "But you started me."

She nodded. Then the smile faded to a ghost and she looked ahead again. She said it was all right, as he said it, which was the way a man would say it. But it was all very abstract, and fine.

"And we don't live in abstractions," she said. "It is all a matter of individuals. And that, the law never understands."

"How can it?" he said, and slowed to circle onto the Parkway. "Law can't be made for individuals, as individuals. There can't be a law for you and a law for me, except in our minds. There has to be one law covering both of us, like a blanket. Maybe our feet will stick out, but—"

He stopped because she was laughing.

"Why, Mr. Weigand!" she said.

He grinned at her, and found that he was not abashed.

"That's what I mean by law," he said. "It only stops me from acting against your law. It doesn't stop me from thinking—unconsciously."

"Well," she said, "it's very nice of you, in a way, Mr.—what is your name, anyway?"

"William," he said. "A distressing name. Or Bill."

"It's very nice of you, Bill Weigand," she told him. "Don't think we girls don't appreciate—"

She let it fall, and Weigand found that her words—or perhaps merely her presence—tingled inside somewhere.

"For God's sake!" Weigand said to himself, in alarmed astonishment. "For God's sake! Is it going to turn out that way?"

He shied off, suddenly.

"The police—" he began, and she turned and laughed at him, for a moment only.

"Don't sound so worried," she said. "I'm not going to divert you." The laughter faded. "Or any policeman," she said, and unexpectedly the bitterness was back in her voice. "For all their fine words, they— hunt people." She was suddenly passionate. "I've seen it, I tell you!" she said. "I've seen it."

Weigand felt that he had climbed slowly up some slippery surface only to slide down it again.

"Right," he said. "I'm sorry, Miss Hunt."

She had not moved, but she seemed to have receded along the seat. His ankle flexed and the foot pressed the accelerator. The car's song heightened and he took it, fast, around two cars toiling along abreast, snapping back into line below the crest of a hill.

"Well," she said, "you don't need to kill us, Mr. Weigand."

He decided that she didn't make sense; that she was already an aggravation. He pointed out, curtly, that he was in a hurry. "After all, I'm a policeman," he said, and the anger in his tone sounded preposterous to himself. She said nothing, but stared ahead. It was all, Weigand told himself without being able to do anything about it, very silly. It remained silly for another thirty miles.

She told him Forty-second and Fifth, because she wanted to stop at the library for a moment. She was out quickly when he stopped by the curb in front of the library lions. As she stood on the sidewalk, closing the door, he was astonished to remember that he had been so peculiarly irritated. She stood with a hand on the door.

"Well," she said, "thank you, Lieutenant."

He was surprised again to find himself speaking.

"I'm sorry," he said. "I seem to have been very irritable. I—well, I'm probably tightened up over the case."

She said she was sure that that was it, and that so, of course, was she.

"Something seems to have got into us," she said, and then she stopped and her eyes widened slowly as they looked into his. Then, for no reason, she started shaking her head. She shook it with a kind of

determination for a moment, and then more slowly and at the end a little doubtfully. Bill Weigand looked at her, and he wasn't irritated at all,
any more, or puzzled. He waited, with a kind of sureness, for her to say
something.

It was a moment before he realized that she was not going to say
anything, which was all right, too. It meant that the thing she was not
going to say was the only thing left to say; that there was no side step
available. There would be time, he thought, to admit what her silence
agreed had eventually to be admitted. Meanwhile he looked at her and
began to smile a little, and thought her eyes widened.

She looked at him a moment longer through widened eyes and then,
with quick grace, she turned away and he watched her run up the steps
toward the library. It occurred to him that he could not remember ever
having seen a woman who looked so attractive, from behind, while
running up stairs. It was, he thought, almost a violation of the laws of
nature.

He watched her until she disappeared through the library doors and
then loop-turned in the avenue to the indignation of several taxicabs
and two buses. He turned right again in Forty-second, thinking about
Dorian, and, to make a left turn in Lexington against a red light and the
law's specific interdiction, let his siren hum faintly. He drove up Lexington a block or two and edged to the curb between two No Parking
signs. Bell, Halpern & Bell had picked themselves a sufficiently over-
powering building.

He found the firm's name in the directory and started toward the ele-
vators. Then he stopped, considering. There was inner amusement in
his eyes as he went, instead, toward a telephone booth. "After all," he
told himself, "if I embody the law, there is no reason why the law
shouldn't embody me, too." He dialed SPring 7-3100. His nickel
returned to the little cup and he pocketed it and told Police Headquar-
ters that Weigand was calling, and wanted to speak to Deputy Chief
Inspector O'Malley, in Homicide. He repeated this desire to O'Malley's secretary. O'Malley came on, gruffly, and said he thought
Weigand was on vacation, for God's sake. Weigand said he had thought
so, too, but that he had run into something.

"Up in Putnam County," he said.

"Jeez, Bill," O'Malley said, relaxing, "how'd you stumble into that?"

Weigand told him. O'Malley said it sounded like quite a business, and Weigand agreed that it was quite a business.

"But," O'Malley reminded him, "you're on leave, remember. So it's nothing to us how you spend it."

That, Weigand said, was the point. Sure enough, he was on leave. "Only," he said, "there are naturally several points in town that need to be checked."

O'Malley made suspicious sounds.

"And," Weigand explained, "if the State Police ask us to cooperate, we'll cooperate, of course. Which might take several men—who aren't on leave. This way, I'm saving the Department a man and—"

O'Malley got it.

"What do you want?" he said.

"Mullins," Weigand told him. "Just Detective Mullins. Can you send him along?"

Inspector O'Malley spluttered for a minute, while Weigand waited politely, as lieutenants must wait while deputy chief inspectors do their spluttering. Then O'Malley said, not too cordially, that he could have Mullins.

"For a day or two," O'Malley warned.

Weigand returned to the switchboard by O'Malley's secretary, got onto Mullins. Mullins was surprised, and when he heard that the Norths were in it broke into words.

"Jeez, Loot," he said. "Is it a screwy one again?"

Weigand said you could call it that, and told Mullins to meet him at Bell, Halpern & Bell's.

· 13 ·

MONDAY
11:40 A.M. TO 1:10 P.M.

The second Mr. Bell—Mr. J. K. Bell, as it turned out—was unavoidably engaged for half an hour, which he trusted would not inconvenience Lieutenant Weigand. Meanwhile, nobody had been in the large office which had belonged to Jean Corbin, or the smaller one which had been Thelma Smith's until five o'clock on the afternoon of Friday, the eighth inst., or been allowed to open the desk in the general office at which Helen Wilson had worked. Possibly the lieutenant would care to occupy his time in one of the offices?

The lieutenant cared. Jean Corbin had worked in a large and just now sunny office, and had had a wide desk facing outward from the windows. Her secretary had had a smaller desk, not facing outward from the windows. Both desks were bare of surface and, within, orderly. Sitting at the big desk, Weigand flipped through papers—typed and annotated advertisements, layouts neatly filed and also annotated; memos printed "From Miss Jean Corbin to . . . ."; pads of yellow paper and lines of sharpened pencils, prepared against the time of creation. And nothing very personal—a box of kleenex; an immaculate and folded towel; a key marked, modestly, "Exec. T." On the desk a

117

fountain-pen set and a memorandum calendar, with "Sat. 9–Sun. 10" virginal on top. Weigand flicked the calendar idly to Monday, wondering what task lay there which would, now, never be performed. There was a single notation:

"Fil. 1–21"

Weigand looked at it thoughtfully, and wondered whether it might apply.

It was, presumably, something which was to have been done, or been remembered, on that day, Monday, September 11. Therefore, presumably, "1–21" did not mean what it at first seemed to mean, unless Miss Corbin had been thinking a good way ahead. "Fil."—whatever "Fil." might be—was not to be encountered on January 21, unless—He flipped to the last sheet on the pad and found it, as he had supposed, to bear the date of December 31. So, naturally, the following January would appear only on the following desk pad; thus any memorandum for a January date might be jotted down anywhere for subsequent transfer. But in that case, why not on the sheet for December 31, which would be torn off last? And, if this cryptic reference was to some engagement for a January which had now, so far as it concerned Jean Corbin, turned grimly mythical, why was he puzzling over it?

"Probably," he thought, "I shouldn't be."

He opened the last drawer in the desk, and was comforted to find less than the perfect order of an efficient executive. Perhaps there, he thought—and found his mind returning to the calendar pad. Lieutenant Weigand, who felt that hunches had value, listened to his hunch.

"All right," he said to himself, "suppose we break it up. Suppose we say that it refers to today."

He waited for his mind to take this bait. His mind blinked at it. Then it brightened. "1" could refer to one o'clock, of course, and, say, indicate a luncheon date. Then—

"Damn," said Weigand, aloud.

Mullins, occupying the doorway and looking every seventy-four inches a policeman in plainclothes, gave a gloomy rumble of agreement.

"Screwy, ain't it?" said Mullins, darkly.

"What?" said Weigand. "What do you think's screwy?"

"Whatever's screwy," Detective Mullins said. "You *look* like it was screwy."

On the contrary, Weigand assured him. It had just straightened out a little.

"Miss Corbin was going to have lunch with someone named Fil. at one o'clock today at Club 21," he said. "What do you think of that?"

"Who's Phil?" said Mullins. "Is he in this?"

Weigand decided that sounds did not convey. He beckoned Mullins, who stared at the memorandum pad.

"Yeh," Mullins said. "Like you said. And, like I said, who's Fil.?"

That, Weigand admitted, they didn't know. Most probably he was nobody they were interested in, or who would do them any good. Mullins looked troubled.

"I thought you said it was straightening out," he protested. "Now you say we don't know who Fil. is and that he probably ain't nobody." He looked at Weigand suspiciously. "Like I say," he said. "Screwy."

"Right," said Weigand, and turned his attention to the open drawer. It was agreeable to have solved even this simple and unimportant cryptogram. And, as Mullins indicated, it left them nowhere. But as he turned to the open drawer, he pulled away the Monday sheet from the pad and put it in his pocket. You never knew.

Jean Corbin evidently had maintained a catchall in the bottom drawer, letting flutter into it such matters of transitory, or uncertain, or merely puzzling, importance as could be committed to paper. There were invitations which she had, Weigand could guess, put off answering and forgotten; there were samples of some material, which might appertain to personal or advertising life. There was a catalogue from a silversmith's, with a cocktail-shaker checked and questioned. There were one or two evidently personal notes, and through them Weigand ran quickly. Then, over one, his eyes moved more slowly, and several times. Then he said, "Well," and showed the note to Mullins. It was addressed: "Dear Jean."

"Dear Jean," it read, "I feel, don't you, that we had better call it off, since evidently it can come to nothing; since neither of us is really willing for it to come to anything? I hope that you will feel this way about it, since I do—quite unmistakably."

It was an odd note and it was signed "J. H. A." This wasn't, Weigand decided, cryptic. It was James Harlan Abel breaking off, rather academically and obscurely until the end and then—"unmistakably."

"Who's this guy?" Mullins said when Weigand pushed the note across the desk to him. "Do we know him?"

Weigand said they did, and named him.

"What was he trying to say?" Mullins wanted to know.

"Well," Weigand said, "he's an English professor, but what he was saying was that he wasn't having any, and no fooling. He was suggesting that she go peddle her papers."

"Yeh," Mullins agreed, after study. "That's what he was trying to say, I guess."

"And," said Weigand, "there's a theory around that if something stuck to Dr. Abel where he didn't want it he'd—well, brush it off. And not care where it fell."

Mullins said it sounded like a screwy theory to him, and whose was it?

"Mrs. North's," Weigand told him. Mullins nodded over the note, in thought.

"Well," he said, "maybe it just sounds screwy, then. I guess we've got our guy."

Weigand's lips crinkled over Mullins' translation from hopelessness to certainty, and said only, "Um-m-m." Then he went on through the desk, and found odds and ends which did not seem to apply. Mullins sat and watched him. Finally Mullins cleared his throat and said he thought it was this Abel guy, all right.

"She was right the other time," Mullins said. "We gotta remember that."

"Right," Weigand said. "We'll remember it."

He lifted the telephone from its cradle on the desk and inquired as to the present condition of the second Mr. Bell. The second Mr. Bell—Mr. J. K. Bell—had recovered from conference and could see Lieutenant Weigand.

Mullins, looking heavily abstracted, started to go along, but he was stopped as, his expression revealed, he had all along feared. He was not to accompany Weigand into the precincts of the second Mr. Bell. He was to go through the desks of Thelma Smith and Helen Wilson and return with what he thought interesting.

"You've read about this case, haven't you?" Weigand inquired, doubtfully.

"Yeh," Mullins said. "On the subway."

He went off to desks, and Weigand went to an even lighter and even larger office, which had corner windows and a large desk facing out from the corner. Mr. Bell, however, was a small man with ruddy cheeks. Funereal gloom overspread his features, appropriately, as Weigand entered. Mr. Bell said it was very sad, wasn't it? Weigand said it was very sad. Mr. Bell immediately smiled and suggested that Lieutenant Weigand would, perhaps, care for a cigar. Lieutenant Weigand indicated that, while deeply appreciative, he would not care for a cigar. Mr. Bell hoped that the lieutenant had found the desks undisturbed as directed. Lieutenant Weigand had.

"Can you," he said, "tell me anything about this?"

He slid the sheet torn from the desk calendar across smooth wood to Mr. Bell, who applied pince-nez and considered.

"No," said Mr. Bell, and slid it back.

"It refers, apparently, to a luncheon engagement at '21' with some person whose name can be abbreviated as 'Fil.,'" Weigand explained. "Do you know any 'Fil.'?"

"No," said Mr. Bell. Then he stopped and the smoothness of his face rippled with cogitation.

"Unless Fillmore," he said. "Jonas Fillmore. But it could hardly be Mr. Fillmore."

"Why?" Weigand wanted to know.

It could hardly be Mr. Fillmore, Mr. Bell explained, because Mr. Fillmore was advertising manager for Carbonated, Incorporated, and Carbonated was not one of their customers. So there would, obviously, have been no reason for Miss Corbin to see Mr. Fillmore.

"Carbonated?" Weigand repeated.

"A soft drink concern," Mr. Bell admitted, with distaste. "Not one of our clients, however."

Something remembered scraped in Weigand's mind, found a door and was admitted.

"They don't make a drink called 'Quench,' do they?" Weigand asked.

Mr. Bell nodded, rather disparagingly.

"And they were clients at one time, weren't they?"

Mr. Bell nodded again, even more disparagingly.

"But there would be no reason whatever for our Miss Corbin to see Mr. Fillmore," Mr. Bell assured him. "No reason whatever."

"Right," Weigand said. "And now can you tell me something about Miss Thelma Smith?"

It took time to get Mr. Bell moving where Weigand wanted him moving, but Weigand took the time. Miss Smith had been with the firm for several years. Yes, she had joined at about the time Miss Corbin accepted a position with them. Yes, certainly Miss Corbin had done rather better with them; she had become an account executive while Miss Smith remained "junior."

"A junior executive?" Weigand asked.

Mr. Bell pursed his lips, thought and nodded. He thought that the term defined Miss Smith's position with the firm; her former position. She was, technically, an assistant office manager, which was, Mr. Bell wanted it clear, a very comfortable position to be in with Bell, Halpern & Bell. But—

"There was some dissatisfaction with her work on the part of several of the executives," Mr. Bell admitted. "Or perhaps it would be more accurate to say 'with her personality.' Mr. Curtis found her very difficult to work with, and some of the others. So we decided that she might be happier elsewhere and—er—accepted her resignation."

"Yes," Weigand said, "as you said. She was fired."

Mr. Bell flushed slightly, looked at Weigand, and finally nodded.

"And how did Miss Corbin feel about that?" Weigand asked. "They were old friends, weren't they?"

"Well," Mr. Bell said, "I suppose they were, in a way. But Miss Corbin quite understood. In fact—"

"In fact, Miss Corbin was one of the executives who had difficulty with Miss Smith's 'personality,' wasn't she?" Weigand suggested. "One of those who recommended that Miss Smith be fired, to be flat about it?"

"Well," Mr. Bell said, "yes. As a matter of fact, she was rather insistent toward the end. Quite surprisingly insistent, some of us thought, since nothing could, after all, be said against Miss Smith's work. But Miss Corbin was much more valuable to us, of course, and when she rather made it an issue—"

They were, Weigand decided as he left Mr. Bell's office a few minutes later, certainly getting on. They were getting on, rather unfortunately, in several different directions, but nobody could deny they were getting places. He remained of this opinion even when Mullins reported that he could discover nothing in either Helen Wilson's or Thelma Smith's desk which seemed to bear. The Smith desk was, in fact, bare of all but undefaced office equipment. In Helen's there was, so far as he could determine, nothing which had personal application. Weigand nodded, and looked at his watch. It was almost twelve-thirty, and it might be a time to catch Mr. Fillmore.

Downstairs, Weigand found a telephone book and afterward a booth, and caught Mr. Fillmore of Carbonated, Inc. Mr. Fillmore was in his office around the corner, and would wait for Lieutenant Weigand if there was something important. About Miss Corbin? He could not imagine how he could help, but he would wait. Weigand and Mullins went around the corner to another formidable building, and rose smoothly in an elevator. Mr. Fillmore was long and thin and looked, Weigand thought, as if his soft drinks disagreed with him.

But he was readily helpful. Miss Corbin had called him the Friday before and suggested lunch that day; when Mr. Fillmore admitted a previous engagement, she fixed Monday. She had not said, directly, why she wanted to lunch with him.

"But you could guess, of course," Weigand prompted.

Fillmore looked at him, and his long face furrowed in a wise smile. He said that he could, certainly, make a guess.

"They wanted to get Quench back, I've no doubt," he said. "Miss

Corbin was, I take it, to have been an advance scout. The agencies keep track of contracts, you know, and our contract for Quench advertising is expiring in a month or so. They may have heard that there is some uncertainty about our renewal."

"With a man named Saunders?" Weigand said.

"Yes," Mr. Fillmore agreed. "With Saunders."

"And is there uncertainty about the renewal?" Weigand asked, while Mullins, sitting in a chair in the corner of the office, nodded wisely. Fillmore stared at Weigand, with lifted eyebrows.

"That isn't properly a police matter, I should suppose," he said. "It is not a matter for general circulation, certainly. But—"

"It won't be circulated, if we can avoid it," Weigand said. "And if we find we can't avoid it, circumstances will have made secrecy unimportant, I imagine."

Fillmore nodded.

"Yes," he said. "I suppose I can guess at the meaning of that. Very well—there is considerable uncertainty about our renewing with Saunders. Very considerable uncertainty."

"And so Miss Corbin might have—made progress?" Weigand asked.

Fillmore was cagey, there. Many things would have entered in; many terms. But, pinned down, he agreed that Miss Corbin might, quite possibly, have started progress.

"Bell, Halpern & Bell is a very good firm, of course," Mr. Fillmore said. "It is certainly one of those we would have considered if we had decided to make a change. Particularly if they had agreed to assign Miss Corbin to the account."

Weigand took it that Miss Corbin was very good.

"Extremely good," Mr. Fillmore said. "She's just done a very strong campaign for Wash-it. A very strong campaign. Quite the talk of the profession, in fact."

Could Weigand take it, then, that the possibility of the account's leaving Saunders for Bell, Halpern & Bell did depend, to a considerable degree, on the assignment of Miss Corbin to the account? Fillmore thought and nodded. And with Miss Corbin dead, the chance of the account remaining with Saunders was, at the least, enhanced? Fillmore hesitated over that one. Finally it appeared that the point was not one on which he would care to commit himself. There were various elements, of which that was, he would go so far as to say, one. "But only one," he assured Weigand. He hoped Weigand would not jump at any conclusions.

"Right," said Weigand. "We'll try not to jump. And thank you."

He collected Mullins, who shook his head gloomily over the situation, said that he had known in advance that it was going to be a screwy one, and inquired if this was one of those they didn't eat on? Weigand saw no reason why it should be. They sat at the counter in the Grand Central and watched oysters bubble in hot milk and butter, consumed well-bubbled oysters contentedly. Mullins said it was sure swell to get back to months with R's in them.

• 14 •

MONDAY
1:10 P.M. TO 4:45 P.M.

Sometime, Weigand thought as he turned the Buick uptown, he would like to have a case which would settle down reasonably—one of those comfortable cases in which suspicion points once, and only once, and all gratified policemen need to do is to prove what they know. Suspicion was a trickster here, more wanton than a weathervane, which at least answered to the wind of the moment. Suspicion whirled with her finger out, pointing everywhere and—nowhere. Unless they all did it together, which was fantastic.

"We've got too many suspects again," he told Mullins. "And too many murders, when you come to that. You read the papers. Which was the essential murder?"

"The essential murder?" Mullins echoed. "Huh?"

"Which came first?" Weigand clarified. "Helen Wilson? Jean Corbin? Whose turn was it, and who merely got in the way?"

"Yeh," said Mullins. "I see what you mean. The Wilson one, I guess. You found it first."

"But the other could have been started any time," Weigand reminded him. "You can set a trap any time."

126

"Yeh," Mullins said. "I guess that one came first, all right."

Mullins was even less than usually helpful, Weigand considered, as he turned through the park. But you couldn't fairly blame him. Weigand wasn't sure that he was being very helpful himself, and wondered how Heimrich was getting on. Was Heimrich being helpful? he wondered. They came out at 110th Street, turned west, then north on Broadway and parked on a street that pierced Columbia University. The office could direct him to Professor Abel's office, and did. Professor Abel's secretary was an earnest young woman in glasses, absurdly what one would have expected. She was sorry that Professor Abel was not in. Weigand expressed sorrow, also. Would he be in today? The secretary thought not. Weigand sighed.

"I wonder if you can tell me where he is?" he asked. The girl looked at him sharply.

"In the country, somewhere," she said.

"Up at Lone Lake, isn't he?"

Weigand was chatty. She looked even more sharply.

"Who are you?" she said. "What do you want to know?"

The defensiveness came too quickly, Weigand decided. If Abel wanted an actress, he should hire an actress.

"William Weigand," he said. "A police lieutenant." He decided to attack. "Dr. Abel telephoned you this morning, didn't he?" he said suddenly.

"No," she said. "That is—yes, I think it was this morning."

"Certainly it was this morning," Weigand told her. "He wanted you to do something for him, didn't he?"

"No," she said. "That is—he merely wanted me to put off some appointments. He told me he might not be back in town for a day or two. He was worried about some appointments."

Weigand wanted to know if she was sure that that was all. He looked rather hard, and she wavered.

"Yes," she said, "of course that was all. What else would there be?"

"All right," Weigand said. "I'll tell you. He has been seeing a good deal of a Miss Corbin lately—Miss Jean Corbin. Does the name mean anything?"

He watched her try to pull herself together, and watched her fail.
She nodded, dumbly.

"I thought it might," he said. "She was killed, you know. And Dr.
Abel had been seeing her frequently, and telephoned you to deny it if
you were asked. Isn't that true?"

"No," she said. "That isn't really true—that is—"

"Well?" said Weigand.

"It was only that he didn't want to be drawn into anything he didn't
have a part in," she said. "He knew it wouldn't help, and his position—
Faculty members can't be drawn into things like that, you know. It—it
is very important to them. And particularly with former students."

"Was Miss Corbin once a student of Professor Abel's?" Weigand
asked.

"Yes," the girl said, unhappily. "Years ago, and he hadn't seen her
for years between, but it—he wouldn't want it talked about. And it
wasn't anything, really."

"You knew because she sometimes called up here?" he prompted.
"Perhaps she came around to pick the Doctor up? And you heard
things from other people?"

She shook her head at first, and then as he continued to look at her
she nodded, unwillingly.

"Only," she said, "it was all over. Really all over." She spoke eagerly, demanding belief. "That's why it would be so unjust if anything
came out and hurt Professor Abel. Because really, he had quit seeing
her entirely."

"Had he?" Weigand said. There was doubt palpable in his voice.
She seized on the doubt.

"Oh, yes!" she said. "It was never anything, really—she was young
and pretty, I suppose, and he enjoyed going places with her. To dinner
and places. He met her again, you know, when he was acting as a con-
sultant for an advertising agency she was connected with. But he
hadn't seen her for weeks."

It came out in a rush, blown along, it was evident, by belief.

"Or only at the camp," the girl said. "But there he couldn't help it,
and there were always others around. He never saw her in town any

more, or took her places." She looked at Weigand anxiously. "I'm sure you'll believe me," she said. "It's really the way I say. Why, for the last two weeks I've been telling her he was out when she telephoned. He told me to say he was out. Doesn't that prove it?"

She was so triumphant about it, as he nodded, that Weigand felt a little ashamed. But she needn't know, of course, that it wasn't helping Abel for her to convince the police that he had broken with Jean Corbin; that it was quite the opposite of helpful. But she needn't know, unless, of course, that small knowledge came to be swallowed up in a much larger, and more devastating, knowledge. He led the questioning downhill to trivialities, thanked her, and collected Mullins. Mullins said he was getting plenty of notes.

"You're sure going to need them," he added, without optimism.

It was after two when they made their next stop, far downtown, and Mullins looked inquiringly at Weigand, who made no move to get out. Then he looked suspicious.

"Right," Weigand said. "Here's where you go to work. Get onto the surrogate's clerk, go through the files, find out all there is to find out about the Brownley fortune. Find out who the heirs are, if it has been determined. And what the status of the litigation is, now. You'll find Helen Wilson on the list as one of the heirs. And there'll be a man named Blair—John Blair. We'll want all there is about them. You can have [he looked at his watch, which said two-twenty] a couple of hours. We're going to start back around five, I hope."

"Back?" said Mullins. Weigand nodded.

"Back to the country, Mr. Mullins," he said. "Back among the crows and the murders. We'll be just in time for a new murder, I expect."

Mullins looked at Weigand, shook his head sadly and got out.

"Hey!" Weigand called after him. "Remember Charles'?"

Mullins nodded.

"We'll meet there about five," Weigand told him. He saw Mullins' face brighten. "Maybe I'll be good for a drink or two," Weigand promised. Mullins disappeared through a revolving door, and even his back seemed to smile approval. Weigand drove to the Criminal Courts building and sent his name in to Assistant District Attorney Fleming.

Fleming said, "Hiya, Bill?" And Weigand said he had his troubles.

"Listen," said Fleming, "didya hear this one? A woman I know lives up in the country and she went into some little A. & P. in the nearest town the other day and asked for truffles. She said: 'Have you got any truffles?' and what do you think he said?" Fleming paused only imperceptibly, taking no chances. "He said, 'Lady, I got plenty, but there's no use talking about them.' Just like that. Pretty quick guy, wasn't he?"

"Very quick," Weigand said. "Very quick indeed. You helped in the Hunt case, didn't you?"

"Hunt?" Fleming said.

"Clayton Hunt," Weigand told him. "Wall Street. Securities. Sing Sing."

"Oh," Fleming said. "That Hunt. Sure."

It had been, Weigand learned, one of those large and popular cases which district attorneys prefer to try in person, but Fleming and another assistant had worked it up, interviewing witnesses and preparing outlines, and sitting in at the trial to question witnesses not likely to excite the press. Thus Fleming had interviewed Helen Wilson and the district attorney had questioned her.

"And her testimony was important?" Weigand said. "For the State, I mean. It helped clinch things, as I recall?"

That, Fleming said, was right. She had been Hunt's confidential secretary, had transmitted his orders and kept his files. And so what she knew was important, when they came to fitting the picture together for the jury.

"Although I don't suppose she knew the importance of the things she was doing when she did them," Fleming said. "The picture could be pieced together only when you were looking for a picture, if you know what I mean. And there was nothing to indicate that she had pieced them together. Until the newspapers began to put it together from the testimony."

"And then did you have trouble with her?" Weigand wanted to know. "I mean, when she began to see where it was leading?"

Fleming said that they hadn't, exactly, had trouble.

"She didn't try to squirm out of anything," he said. "Out of any definite fact, that is. She wasn't happy about it, or cooperative beyond the mere facts, but the jury could see that and it all helped—helped us, that is. Made what she testified all the more convincing."

Weigand nodded, and said there was another point.

"Did you," he asked, "gather that there was something between her and Hunt? Something more than transmitted orders and letters taken and the like?"

Fleming thought a moment and then shook his head, slowly.

"Not what you mean," he said. "On her part, anyway—and, to give him credit, on his. That's only what I felt, of course. It wasn't to our advantage to dig anything up. Impeach her testimony. And the other side, naturally, wouldn't bring it up. But my impression, for what it's worth, is that the thing was on the up and up, as far as that sort of thing was concerned."

He nodded, confirming his impression to himself.

"Of course," he said, "it may not have been all business between them. I got the impression that she felt a lot of admiration for him, that sort of thing. I think her father was dead?" Weigand nodded. "Well, she may have thought of Hunt as—not a father, of course, but somebody who would fill the lesser roles of a father. I'm just guessing; I don't know whether it helps."

Weigand nodded that it helped.

"As a matter of fact," Fleming said, "I liked the girl—an honest sort of girl. It's too bad about her."

"Yes," Weigand said. "I think it's too bad. And did Hunt feel—fatherly, toward her, do you suppose?"

Fleming shook his head and said he wouldn't know. There was nothing to show about that, he said.

"But he seemed to be an all right sort of guy in other ways," Fleming said. "A crook, obviously, but otherwise a decent enough citizen. Family man—all that sort of thing. Really meant it, too, I'd guess."

"Did his family have any particular contact with Helen Wilson—during the trial, I mean?" Weigand asked.

Fleming shook his head. Mrs. Hunt and her daughter had been in court, of course, and heard Helen's testimony, but he didn't know of any contact. They had—but wait a minute. There was one thing he'd seen. Helen had finished testifying early in the afternoon and the luncheon recess was taken immediately, and everybody poured out into the rotunda of the Supreme Court building. And there Mrs. Hunt and her daughter, in the crowd, had come face to face with Helen Wilson, who was being escorted out of the building by one of the assistant district attorneys. Things were looking bad for Hunt, by that time, and his wife and daughter showed it.

"The daughter especially," Fleming said. "She was white, you know—strained-looking. I don't know if you've seen her?"

"Yes," Weigand said. "I've seen her."

"Nice-looking," Fleming said. "Only not then—or maybe then too, in a way. But sort of frozen and hopeless, and having trouble with control, if you know what I mean. Well, she and Helen Wilson came almost face to face."

"And what happened?" Weigand said.

"Well," Fleming said, "nothing happened, really. The Wilson girl was disturbed and unhappy, because the picture was clear enough by then and the importance of the pieces she had given us, and when she saw the Hunts she hesitated and I thought she was going to say something. And—"

"And?" Weigand said.

It was, Fleming said, only a feeling. Helen Wilson had started to say something and looked at the Hunt girl's face and hesitated and flushed. And the Hunt girl—

"Well," he said, "she just looked through Wilson. Nothing you could put a finger on; no rebuff you could put into words. But it made Helen feel like two cents—two cents' worth of Judas, if you know what I mean. Unjust, too, as it happened, but you could see how the Hunt girl might feel." He paused, recalling the situation. "Funny thing," he said. "I heard the two girls became rather good friends. I wouldn't have thought it, from that day. Although there was no real reason why they shouldn't, of course, after it was all over."

Weigand drew deeply on his cigarette and ground it out.

"Well," he said, "thanks."

"Help?" Fleming asked.

"I don't know," Weigand said. "It might."

Weigand felt a little submerged, driving uptown toward his next stop. "It might help," he said to himself, but he couldn't get away from it. It might at that—hell! He swerved to the curb in Park Avenue, just below the Grand Central, and was gruff with a doorman who tried to assure him that he could not park in front of the entrance. "The hell I can't," Weigand assured him. He confirmed that this was the address he had got at Bell, Halpern & Bell, and told a uniformed man on the switchboard that he wanted the superintendent. He told the superintendent that he wanted to examine the apartment which had been Jean Corbin's. The superintendent read the newspapers too, it appeared; anyway, Weigand's displayed shield was persuasive.

"This," Weigand thought, "will probably be a fool's errand."

It was a very large building, but it was a very small apartment—one moderate-sized room, a depression for a serving-pantry, a bath and dressing-room. The closet was full of clothes; very nice-looking clothes, and the closet was aromatic with dying scent. It wasn't pleasant to think of the girl who had owned the clothes, as Weigand had last seen her. And what could the clothes tell him? That she had been pretty, and gaily busy of nights; that she had made money and spent it, and known the good places to go for clothes. All of which he knew.

The slender, neatly kept desk told him no more, except that Jean Corbin had been orderly in small matters. There was a stack of bills under a paperweight, and none was overdue. They looked as if they had been stacked up for payment. There was a checkbook lying nearby and the neat tabulations on its counter-foils indicated a healthy, if unswollen, balance. Weigand riffled through the stubs, expecting nothing sensational—and found nothing sensational. He looked around the room, and felt the girl who had, so finally, gone out of it. Modern and quick and polished she had been, immaculate and assured. Her impression on the room was light, but defined; she had left it in the material of fabrics, in the moderated brightness of lamp-shades, in magazines on a table near the telephone. And her death had been so very ugly.

It was getting him nowhere, but it was routine gone through. Obscurely, he felt that the atmosphere of the room completed his picture of Jean Corbin—that there was now nothing new to be learned about her which would be significant to his purpose. She had kept a light, assured hand on things, and somewhere the hand had slipped; somewhere she had met a person who was not light and assured, but rough and angry. And it might be that, ironically, it was nothing more than accident; that all this poise had been shattered by something which, so far as she was concerned, was as senseless and unordered as an avalanche. He turned a mental page and locked the door of Jean Corbin's apartment behind him, and left the key at the telephone desk.

The doorman was helpful, now, and full of deference. He moved into the street and held up a staying hand while Weigand swung his car and headed south down Park and Fourth. Weigand swung through Fourteenth to Fifth, and turned through disorderly streets near the Washington Arch. Perry Street. He slid along it looking at numbers and found one. There was no doorman here, forbidding encroachment. It was with some difficulty that he found the janitor who could let him into Helen Wilson's apartment on the top floor of an old house. He climbed dark, carpeted stairs behind the janitor, who had also read the newspapers and was willing to talk. So far as Weigand could determine, the janitor had nothing of importance to say. The Wilsons had been mighty fine people, and easy to please.

"Mrs. Wilson and her daughter?" Weigand said. "They both lived here, then?"

"In winters," the janitor said. "Just in winters. Mrs. Wilson spends the summers out at that place in the country, and the girl commutes."

He opened the door and showed an inclination to remain. Weigand told him he needn't. The apartment, even at four o'clock of September afternoons, was shadowy. Weigand switched on the lights from a tumbler just inside the door. Lamps glowed and sidelights by a fireplace. It was an easy, comfortable room, with windows on the long shadows of the street. There was easy, comfortable furniture in it, and a daybed. Behind there was another room, evidently Mrs. Wilson's, and to one side a kitchen. There was a bath next to the kitchen.

The desk was not so neat, nor the bills so recently paid or so large. Nor, in their closet off the hall, were the clothes so gently shining or bearing such superior names. Everywhere there was simplicity and—Weigand thought for a word. Friendliness. People left impress on their rooms. You could sit in this one, and stretch your legs, and smoke and talk, and pull a chair near for your feet. There was a low bookcase along one wall. Weigand completed his inspection of the desk pigeon-holes to no advantage and opened the drawer beneath. The drawer bulged with photographs—photographs of Helen and of her mother at the camp, of others—there was a picture of the Norths playing tennis, and one of Dorian Hunt. Weigand looked at it. Dorian was sitting on the ground, with her brown knees drawn up and held between her hands, and she was looking back at the camera and laughing. It was taken at a camp somewhere, by the costume of shirt and shorts. There was a picture of Van Horst, standing beside a woman whom Weigand could not place; and there were half a dozen pictures, bound together by rubber bands, taken somewhere else—in Florida, at a guess. All of people he had never seen before except—yes, there was Mrs. Wilson, smiling a little self-consciously among men and women who were, for the most part, much younger.

He laid the pictures on the shelf of the desk as he looked at them, working down through the layers. Then he held a picture and stared at it and laid it down on the desk and leaned back in his chair, staring at the ceiling. So Clayton Hunt was Helen's "most affectionately," was he? And what was he to deduce from that? Distant avuncular fondness? Indulgent employer to admiring aide? Or—

Leaning back, he stiffened, and then eased his chair's legs to the floor. The soft sound was repeated outside. Somebody was coming up the stairs which led only to the Wilson apartment—coming very quietly, without announcement. There was the faintest of footfalls on the landing before Weigand moved, quickly, to the light switch, praying that the door fitted closely; thankful that it opened inward and against the wall where he was standing. The lights were out as he moved again, through the shadows and quickly, and he had escaped from the danger-ous proximity to the switch—where the hand of the intruder would first come groping—before he heard a key sliding gently into the lock. He was across the living-room and into the bedroom beyond and had shut the communicating door almost to behind him before the key turned with a tiny, clicking sound, and the apartment door began to open.

The door opened inward slowly, for a moment screening the intruder. Weigand's muscles tightened with his nerves. His breath came in softly to fill his lungs, and he could feel a prickling at the back of his neck. Then the door was fully opened and Weigand's breath came out again in a soundless sigh.

Dorian Hunt stood in the doorway. For a moment she stood hesitant, her eyes traveling around the room. Then she was moving, quickly and with a grace which the man watching wished desperately he might forget, toward the opened desk.

She stopped there, as he had known she would, and across the room he could hear her quickly-drawn breath. For a moment she stood, action frozen, one hand outstretched toward the rifled desk. Only her eyes moved for that moment, and then the body turned slowly. And then the instant broke, and there was a flow of movement in the girl which carried her back toward the door. Then Weigand spoke, and the harshness in his voice startled him.

"Well, Miss Hunt?" he said.

His voice checked her. She turned, facing him, as he came through the door from the bedroom. Her hands clenched as they hung by her sides.

"Well," he said, "that's better. You wouldn't rush off, would you?"

His voice was cold, scathing. Anger and color flared in her face.

"Why shouldn't I leave?" she said, and her voice was high and shook a little. "Can you stop my leaving?"

Weigand's answer was immediate and unspoken. He crossed to the door behind her, closed it and stood against it. She turned to face him, and they stood close together. He could see her breast rising and falling quickly.

"What did you come here for, Miss Hunt?" he said. "What are you looking for?"

He saw her breast rise as she drew in a steadying breath. He waited;

saw her catch control. She was acting well, he thought, when the anger faded out of her face.

"You startled me," she said. "I'm sorry I seemed—excited, I felt—I felt as if you had trapped me."

She was disarming, now, but Weigand stared at her and his expression did not change.

"Well," he said, "haven't I? Aren't you trapped, as you put it?"

She laughed. It almost sounded like laughter.

"But it's ridiculous," she said. "I came here because Mrs. Wilson asked me to, and you make me feel—you make me feel as if I had been caught in something criminal. Or you did."

"Yes," Weigand said. "You might feel that way. Why did Mrs. Wilson ask you to come here?"

He saw the story growing behind her eyes; felt that she knew he saw it growing. There was hesitation too brief to be perceived, but not too brief to feel, in her answer.

"She wanted me to pick up something for her," Dorian Hunt said. "She said that, if I got down this way, it would be kind if I would pick up Helen's checkbook—hers and Helen's, rather—and bring it out with me. I said I would be glad to if I got downtown and—"

"And you got downtown," Weigand said. "I see. And then you decided to leave without taking the checkbook."

"But of course," she said. "Anybody would. I saw that somebody had been going through the desk and I thought I heard breathing and I—well, I was terrified. Why shouldn't I be? How was I to know that it was—that it was the beneficent, guarding police?"

There was irony which tried to be light irony in the last phrase. Weigand let it slide past him. She waited, and saw that it slid past him.

"Well," she said, "are you going to believe me? Or is that too simple for the police mind?"

"Yes," he said. "That is too simple for the police mind. Or too complicated. No, I don't think I'm going to believe you, Miss Hunt. Because, you see, I think I know what you came after. I think you came after a picture—a picture of your father, inscribed to Helen Wilson. I think you didn't want anybody to know you had come, and came up the stairs very quietly. I think you—where did you get the key, Miss Hunt?"

He snapped the question at her.

"Mrs. Wilson gave it to me, of course," she said. "As I told you. And I don't know what you mean about the picture."

He listened to her voice. He thought she did know about the picture.

"What do you think the picture means, Miss Hunt?" he asked. "I was wondering when I heard you outside. I was wondering if it meant anything. What do you think, Miss Hunt?"

"Nothing," she said. "It doesn't mean—"

She broke off. He was smiling a little, not happily.

"All right!" she said. "All right! So I did come after the picture—to keep it away from snoopers. From snooping policemen—from people who would give it to the newspapers, and make it seem like something it wasn't; would drag it all out again . . . and again . . . and again! To keep it out of the garbage-can of minds like yours, if you want to know. So what are you going to do about it, Lieutenant? Wouldn't you like to lock me up because I came to get a picture my father gave to a girl who thought he was a fine man? Wouldn't you—"

There were tears in her voice now. But they were angry tears.

"He *was* a fine man!" she said. "You wouldn't know about men like that—you want to hound them, and twist what they do, and send them to prison." She flared at him. "Send me to prison, why don't you?" she said, and her voice was shaking. "Why don't you? You've caught me, haven't you? You can charge me with something, can't you? You're stronger than I am—why don't you take me away and lock me up? Isn't that what policemen are for, Lieutenant Weigand? To lock people up?"

Weigand felt tired, suddenly. There was tiredness in his voice.

"I don't want you for anything, Miss Hunt," he said. "I don't want the picture for anything. If you're lying about it, I'll find out. You can go any time, Miss Hunt." He watched her a moment. When he spoke again there was something bitter in the weariness of his voice.

"And take your damned picture with you," he said. His voice was level, tired and bitter. He left the door, suddenly, and moved across to the desk. He picked up the picture, slowly, unemotionally, and held it out to her.

"Take your picture," he said.

She hesitated a moment, and there was an odd change in her face. Then, without saying anything, she reached out and took the picture. She looked at it a moment and then her fingers loosened and she let it drop between them. She looked at him a moment longer and then turned. And then she was gone and the door was closed behind her and he heard her steps going down the stairs, not trying to be silent. He stood and looked at the picture and after a while he said he would be damned. He said it reflectingly, as if he were puzzled. Then, without touching the picture, he went to the door and out of the apartment and found the janitor and gave him the key. He had nothing to say to the janitor, who had conversation left. He wanted to look up the street to see if Dorian Hunt was still in it, but instead he looked ahead of him as he climbed into his car. He drove without thinking through the maze of streets, came out on Sixth Avenue and stopped in front of Charles'.

There was a seat at the bar and the bartender smiled and nodded toward it. Then, looking at Weigand's face, he said nothing, but poured a jigger of gin in a mixing-glass and added vermouth. Weigand groped for the martini without looking at it, and drank it, staring into the mirror in the center of the oval bar.

• 15 •

MONDAY
4:45 P.M. TO 7:10 P.M.

The bartender had a benign pink face and knew everybody. He was merely present if Weigand wanted to say anything until Weigand finished his drink, and edged the glass back across the bar. The bartender picked it up and twirled it between his fingers.

"I tell you, Lieutenant," he said, "you never tasted my sherry martini, did you?"

"What?" said Weigand. "No. Sherry martini?"

The bartender smiled, approvingly. He said that was right. Sherry martini.

"You ought to try it sometime, Lieutenant," he said. He hesitated, as if making a decision; acting a little for Weigand's distraction. "I tell you," he said. "Suppose I mix you one now? I'd just like to have you try it."

"Why, yes," Weigand said. "Sure, I'd like to try it."

The bartender went to the other side of the bar and came back with a bottle. He showed the label to Weigand.

"This is about the only kind you ought to use," he explained. He was serious and friendly about it. "It has to be as dry as you can get it—

140

almost white, see? It's too expensive to serve regularly, of course, but I think you'd like to try it."

"Yes," Weigand said. Now his eyes were focused again, and the bartender nodded hardly perceptible approval to himself. "You use it instead of vermouth?"

The bartender beamed, and said that Weigand had it.

"Same proportions," he said. "Same everything." His hand swooped out of sight and came back with a mixing-glass again. The glass burrowed into ice, and came up almost full. "You've got to measure it," the bartender said, earnestly. "Trouble with most people's drinks, they think they don't have to measure them." A look of pain crossed the friendly, pink features. "I'll tell you," he said, "there are some men behind bars right here in New York—!" He left the conclusion hanging, unable to encompass the enormity in words. "Twenty-five years I've been mixing drinks," he said. His eyes saddened. "With an interval, of course," he admitted. "I wouldn't try to mix anything without measuring. Not anything." He cast around in his mind. "Not an old-fashioned," he assured Weigand. "No, sir. Not even an old-fashioned."

He mixed as he talked. Gin poured into the hourglass jigger and fell on ice in the shaker. The jigger reversed itself. Sherry filled it until surface tension strained to hold it in the measure. It joined the gin. A spoon whirled, spinning in trained fingers. It was soothing, diverting to watch the spoon, Weigand found. A clean glass; a big olive. The martini shook in through a strainer. It slid across to Weigand, who had to lift it slowly to maintain the tension, which was now transferred to the glass. It was a game. He sipped, and the bartender watched, pink face expectant, consoling.

Weigand's eyebrows went up and his head moved, appreciatively nodding. As if it, too, had been held by surface tension, the bartender's face broke out of expectancy. A smile appeared. The dignified head with its pink crown nodded, too.

"I tell you," the bartender said, "there's nothing like it. Not in a martini."

It had an aromatic, elusive taste. Weigand, fully engrossed, tried another sip. It was hard to define the difference, but it was a fine difference. It was a clearer taste, at once more gentle and more decisive. If a thing could be more gentle and at the same time more decisive.

"Right," Weigand said. "It's something, all right." He tasted again. "It's certainly something," he said.

"Yes, sir," the bartender said. "It makes a mighty fine martini." He let his assurance sink in. "But you've got to be careful," he said. His voice was warning. "Not just any sherry. It's got to be dry. I mean *dry*." He looked horrified at a thought which silently crossed his mind. "Not domestic!" he warned. "Don't think you can do it with *domestic!*" His voice was urgent, and he looked at Weigand anxiously, for reassurance.

"Right," Weigand said. It seemed pretty important to him, too. "I won't use domestic." He found that he was uttering "domestic" with a kind of alarm, almost of loathing. The bartender nodded before him and then his gaze shifted to the next stool. It lost a little of its avuncular warmth.

"Hiya, Loot," Detective Mullins said, from the next stool. "Hiya, pal." This was to the bartender, who looked faintly abashed. "Old-fashioned, I guess." The bartender winced, but was too much a gentleman to show it. Weigand was amused, he discovered. Two martinis elevated amusement from a sub-cellar of consciousness.

"Well," he said: "Mr. Mullins. In person. Have a drink, Mr. Mullins."

He shifted to observe Mr. Mullins, who observed him.

"Sure," Mullins said. "Why not? An old-fashioned, I guess."

"This," said Weigand, "is where you came in. Did you get the dope?"

"Yeh," Mullins said. "I got the dope. And of all the—"

"Right," Weigand said. "Did you find the people—Helen Wilson, John Blair?"

Mullins had. It had been a hard job. He had had to go through—

"Right," Weigand said. "And how about it?"

Mullins started to haul out what was evidently an encyclopedia of notes. Weigand stopped him.

"Hold onto all that," he said. "In case. But just tell me."

Well, Mullins said, it was like the Loot thought, or he guessed it

#11   11-13-2020 11:24AM
Item(s) checked out to ELLITON, JOHN S..

TITLE: Murder out of turn
DUE DATE: 12-04-20

Central 979-7151 on the web at jmrl.org
    or call Toll-free 1-866-979-1555

was. Like in the newspapers, anyway. Helen Wilson had been in line to inherit plenty from the Brownley estate.

"Plenty?" Weigand repeated. "Such as what?"

That Mullins couldn't answer. The estate had not yet been appraised; there was evidence of a good many bad investments. All anybody could be sure of was that there would be plenty. "What I'd call plenty, anyway," Mullins amplified.

"Right," Weigand said. "We'll call it plenty, for the moment, anyway."

Helen inherited through her father and absolutely. Dying before final adjudication, her share went to the next of kin. If she had lived to receive the money, it would have gone to her heirs—or to anyone to whom she had willed it. But now—

"Yes," Weigand prompted. "Now?"

Now it went to three people. John Blair—Weigand nodded over that confirmation—a chap named Archibald Blair who was—"Right," Weigand said. "We can go into that later, if we need to." And a man named William Simpson, who also was—

"Right," Weigand said. "It checks, as you said."

He stared at his empty glass, but shook his head as the bartender also regarded it, questioningly. Mullins finished his own drink and thrust it forward hurriedly. The bartender, a little gloomily, mixed another old-fashioned. Weigand stared at his glass, but now there was a different sort of abstraction in his stare.

"Only," Weigand said, at length, "it was Blair who got slugged. I'm afraid that's a catch." He looked at Mullins' glass. "Drink it up," he said. "We're moving along."

Mullins drank it up, looking disappointed, as might a man with more old-fashioneds in his mind. Weigand pushed bills across the bar and reapproved the sherry martini. He would watch out about domestic, he promised. The bartender nodded and smiled and was clearly pleased with Weigand's progress. The bartender was a physician, surveying convalescence. Weigand checked his watch with the clock over the door, and they agreed, substantially, that it was five thirty-five.

An hour and a half to Lone Lake, if they drove fast; an hour and three-quarters if traffic was bad. Suddenly, unexpectedly, either time seemed too long. Weigand was, to his own surprise, conscious of an unaccountable feeling of urgency. He shook his head, but the feeling persisted—a feeling that he had already been too long away from the lake, and the people there; that it was necessary that he be there, quickly.

Weigand slid behind the wheel and started with a jerk which surprised Mullins, beside him. They swung quickly west, through traffic. "If Mullins weren't along, I'd be using the siren," he thought, obscurely, and was mildly astonished at the thought. But Mullins could not be encouraged in a vice. They climbed the ramp to the express highway and paid little attention to the signs which said "35 M.P.H." They even wove in and out, now and then, circling slow cars, taking all advantages. Weigand said little until, beyond the highway and the Henry Hudson Parkway, past the bridge over the Harlem, they settled down to an unvarying fifty on the Saw Mill River Parkway. It was merely a question, now, of letting the road roll back.

"Well, Loot," Mullins said, conscious of a relaxation of tensity, "how do you figure it? Is it a screwy one?"

It was a familiar opening move between them. It invited Weigand to analyze; to rub his thoughts against the substantial common sense of Detective Mullins. It was time for that, Weigand thought, if it was ever going to be. He slid lower in the seat; the speedometer needle climbed to fifty-five. The sun slanted from the left and from behind and traffic thinned on the road. A motorcycle policeman, coming toward them, turned in his seat to watch the car, tried to intercept the driver's eyes in warning, abandoned the project. Weigand swerved in to pass a plodding, ancient Pierce-Arrow; swerved back to the outside lane.

"Yes," he said, "it's screwy—screwy with an extra turn. It's twin-screwy."

"Jeez!" said Mullins, appreciatively.

Weigand waited a moment to give Mullins time to complete his appreciation of the grimness of circumstances. He held the inside lane, going fast, at the Cross-county Parkway intersection, and gained speed as they passed on the eminence above Yonkers. They went downhill and into a broad curve at a speed which made Mullins look inquiringly at his lieutenant. Weigand was staring ahead, and his eyes did not shift as he began to talk.

The problem, he told Mullins, was, at the start, a problem of two simultaneous murders—simultaneous, that was, to appearance. But the probability that they were distinct murders, having no causal relation to each other, was, Weigand thought, faint. Coincidence seldom went that far.

"Yeh," Mullins said, "they're hooked up, I guess."

Then, if you assumed they were hooked up, you could assume that one had been committed to cover up the other. Thus you could call one the essential murder and the other the superficial murder.

"Huh?" said Mullins, toiling.

Weigand slowed impatiently for a red light; was moving again before it quite changed.

One murder, if Mullins liked that better, was a primary murder, which would have occurred regardless of the other. But the second murder could not occur until there had been a first.

"Yeh," said Mullins. "Only which is first? I don't get it."

That, Weigand said, was the rub, and it rubbed harder because there seemed to be motives for both murders. And rubbed harder still because, although the body of Helen Wilson had been the first found, there was no evidence to show whether she had been killed before or after the trap was laid for Jean Corbin, who might merely have died later but, so far as they were concerned, have been murdered first.

Mullins looked hopelessly at Weigand, and shook his head.

"Right," Weigand said. "I know how you feel. So do I—or so did I."

So, he went on, as the speedometer needle climbed to sixty and stayed there, you had to make at least two distinct assumptions to begin. First, you could assume that Helen Wilson's murder was the essential murder, starting there because hers was the first body found. Then you could find suspects. You did find suspects.

"Yeh," said Mullins. "This Blair guy."

Obviously, Weigand agreed, first of all this Blair guy. He had the best of motives—money. He had opportunity, as, apparently, did everybody else. And he was fine, until he got slugged. That tore it, or seemed to. There was a chance, of course, that he was still the murderer. He repeated to Mullins his speculations on that point, first formulated with the Norths as audience. Mullins thought it over, and shook his head.

"Fancy," he said. "You *could* argue that way, but it's pretty fancy."

"Right," Weigand said. "I agree, I think."

Then, assuming that there was not something they had missed—"and I think we've got everything of importance," Weigand interjected—there was only one remaining suspect for the Wilson murder as the essential murder. That was Dorian Hunt. Weigand's tone remained emotionless. But the car's pace suddenly increased.

Dorian Hunt had opportunity, like the rest. It was difficult to think that any woman could have been Blair's assailant, but not impossible. The women were dressed as efficiently as the men at the lake; one of them armed with, say a tire iron—

"Was that what they used?" Mullins asked.

Weigand admitted that they didn't know, except that it was something made of iron, and in the shape of a bar. There had been rust particles in Blair's wound. A tire iron would serve, for the argument; a woman might use it, although it was not characteristic, admittedly. But, neither was murder.

And Dorian Hunt might have motive. It was not clear, reasonable motive like Blair's. It argued emotional instability of some sort—"as what murder doesn't?" Weigand interrupted himself. It argued a period of brooding over Clayton Hunt's trial and imprisonment, and a fixation of blame on Helen Wilson. But both these things were entirely possible.

"She's high strung, at any rate," Weigand said. "She has a good deal of what you might call emotional intensity. I'll admit she seems, at bottom, balanced enough. But I'll also admit I'm no psychiatrist."

"It could be," Mullins said. "We've known it to happen that way."

They had, Weigand agreed. It was unusual, but not unheard-of. But then, anything was unusual as a motive, except money and, in one of its forms, jealousy. They seemed to rule the murderer's roost.

"Anybody else for Wilson?" Mullins said, to start things again. Weigand did not answer immediately, because the light ahead turned red. The speed of the car checked; then the Buick rolled free again as the brakes were released. The lonely, angry cry of the siren rose from the car hood's interior, and Mullins jumped involuntarily. Then he looked curiously at Weigand, as the car, dodging a quickly halted bus, rolled on and picked up speed.

"We're in a hurry, huh?" he said.

"Yes," Weigand said. "We're sort of in a hurry."

He was glad that Mullins did not ask why. Weigand was not sure he knew why. But there was something in his mind commanding speed; ordering that obstacles to speed be brushed aside.

"Yes," said Weigand. "That seems to be all for Helen. So we make our next supposition—that she was killed because she knew something about the plan to kill Jean Corbin. And that, I think, begins to fit in."

It fitted in only as he talked, and remembered—that was one of the advantages of talking it out. Helen Wilson had left the North cabin Saturday afternoon to go to the store—and to go to Jean Corbin's cabin to leave something. A tennis shirt, or something, Weigand remembered. And there you had the likeliest time for her to stumble onto something—onto, why, of course, the murderer switching the cans! Or, probably, getting ready to switch the cans, and being in the cabin with his presence unexplained.

"Sure enough," Mullins said. He looked at the lieutenant admiringly. "And," he said, "that pins down the time the murderer set the trap."

It did. He had set the trap then—well, sometime between, say, four-thirty and five, or five and five-thirty, or any half-hour period within those times, on Saturday afternoon. And Helen Wilson had stumbled onto him and—

"He probably gave some excuse," Weigand said. "Something that sounded reasonable enough at the time, but would sound mighty thin to Helen when Jean was killed; something she would remember, then, and tell. So, instead of calling the whole thing off, which would have been the other alternative, he let it go ahead, but killed Helen so that she could never tell of having seen him there. And that—"

Weigand paused, thinking. The car hesitated at Hawthorne circle, shot around the curve with the tires protesting, and straightened out on the Bronx River Extension. There was the sudden splatter of a motorcycle engine behind. Weigand didn't look back. Instead, the siren on the Buick spoke gently, in remonstrance. The motorcycle came alongside and the policeman on it took a look. The siren murmured again, and Weigand nodded to the motorcycle man. The motorcycle dropped back.

"—and that," Weigand said, "tells us another thing. For some reason, it was important that the murder occur that day. It couldn't be postponed."

He paused, conscious of insecurity in that statement, and waited for Mullins.

"Yeh," Mullins said. But he said it doubtfully. "Only—"

"Yes?" Weigand encouraged.

"Well, Loot," Mullins said. "It looks to me like that doesn't have to be so. Say she saw somebody in the cabin who wouldn't normally be there, because if she didn't she wouldn't think anything about it, see?"

Weigand nodded.

"Well, then," Mullins said. "Wouldn't she maybe remember having seen this guy—or this dame, whichever it was—after the Corbin girl got bumped, no matter *when* the Corbin girl got bumped? Even if he called off the killing then, and did it later, wouldn't she get to thinking about it, and remember that it had looked sorta funny for this guy to be around that afternoon and then, maybe—"

Mullins stopped, entangled in prose, but pretty certain that Weigand would get him. Weigand got him, it appeared. Weigand nodded doubtfully, and then more confidently and, Mullins decided, in approval.

"Right," Weigand said, finally. "We'll leave that open. But we'll suppose that Helen was killed because she saw something that afternoon. Right?"

"Yeh," Mullins said. "I guess that's right, all right."

So then they looked for suspects of the murder of Jean Corbin, taking it as the essential murder. They looked for suspects, and found plenty.

There was Blair, again—jealousy, this time, on the assumption that Jean was easing him off for Professor James Harlan Abel. And Abel, on the same assumption, because—

"Listen, Loot," Mullins, encouraged by his success, cut in. "This girl Jean was a good-looker, wasn't she? Something you'd expect a guy to go for, even a professor? So why would he be bumping her off?"

Weigand shook his head, this time. You had to see Abel differently, he thought. You had to see him as a self-centered man, narrowly, intensely, living life as he planned it, and ruthlessly eliminating invasions. You could add to that the fact that, as a faculty member, his position might be imperiled if it came out that he, married, was in a close association with a much younger woman who had, moreover, formerly been a student of his. Then, to these, you could add a certain coldness, a rather singular detachment, you felt in the man. When you added them together the sum was—possible suspect.

"Yeh?" said Mullins, doubtfully. Weigand nodded, decisively. "O.K., Loot," Mullins said, bowing to superior insight.

You had, also, Saunders, who had once also been a very intimate associate of Jean's, who had left the advertising agency, as a result of Jean's machinations. You might assume that he had found out that Jean Corbin was lunching with Fillmore that day—Monday—and that her purpose was to get the Quench account back, as apparently it was. So there you had a combination of growing anger over a period of years, jealousy perhaps, and immediate need to intervene.

"Yeh," Mullins said. "That's a good, solid one, all right."

It might be, Weigand admitted. But it was no solider than Blair's for killing Helen Wilson—not as solid, really. It might very well be feebler, counting personalities, than Abel's or, to bring in another, Mrs. Abel's. There you had good, straightforward jealousy and, moreover, a personality which fitted better than Saunders'.

"Saunders is one of these hearty guys," Weigand explained. Mullins nodded.

"Of course," he said, "sometimes it *is* the hearty guys."

"Sometimes," said Weigand, "it's almost anybody. But the hearty guys are pretty well down."

Weigand drove for a good many minutes before he said anything more. He turned from the Bronx River Extension onto Route 100, branched from it to the tortuous wanderings of the Pines Bridge Road along the reservoirs. He was making good time, the car clock told him—only a little more than an hour to Pines Bridge. The twisting of the road slowed him, somewhat. It was, Mullins said after a long time, a screwy road.

Weigand's thoughts, he discovered, had switched from the issue at hand. He was remembering the drive in that morning with Dorian— along here, somewhere, he had been arguing with her about policemen. A little farther along she had startled him, and very possibly saved them from a bad smash, by warning him of the curve—the first of the "curves"; the one that was there. He found himself watching for the curve, where they had for an instant shared alarm; where, for the split part of a second, their lives had been cupped together in a moment of danger, which had passed almost before it could be realized. He saw several curves which might be it, and then one he knew was.

It might, he saw, as they went around it in the reverse direction, have been a very nasty smash, although probably not a fatal one. The main road, in the direction they had been going, turned at right angles to the left, and another road—apparently little used—came in at the right. In the "Y" there was a triangle of rough, but reasonably solid, gravel. You might skid in that gravel and come out all right; you might skid through it and pile up against the bank beyond. It was hard to tell what a car would do—you might even miss the bank and slide farther right, where it shelved away into a fairly deep ditch. That would be the big danger, of course. You—

But the point was, of course, that they had done nothing of the kind, but merely slowed decorously and rounded the curve safely. Thanks to her cry. So it had, in fact, been nothing at all. He wrenched his mind away from it, and from Dorian. When he began to speak again, it was of Thelma Smith. It was hard to make Mullins understand Thelma Smith—the excited bitterness she had showed against Jean Corbin, the string of grievances which had poured so angrily from her; the mingling of hate and love that you could, if you wanted, read into her outburst.

"Well," Mullins said, "she sure sounds like quite a dame." He thought a moment. "It looks to me, Loot," he said, "like she's the one we're after."

It could be, Weigand said. Or, by some stretch of the imagination, and a willingness to assume there was more to know than they knew, Bram Van Horst. Or even, assuming there was everything still to know, the fat menace of old Marvin, who sold wood but no kindling, and indignantly mowed for a man whose character he blackened with evident glee. But Weigand added these last names idly.

He completed the last turn of the Pines Bridge Road impatiently, and the car's speed picked up on the hilly straightaway to Somers. Mullins was puzzled again by their speed. He had never known the Loot to drive so fast, except when there was a reason for fast driving clearly in sight. And Weigand, even as he pressed harder on the accelerator pedal, was puzzled to account for the nagging insistence of that something in his mind which kept saying, "Faster! Faster!"

And then the nagging, after Somers was past, and after they were on Route 22, and through Brewster on the last stretch to Lone Lake, changed somewhat in character. It was a kind of buzzing in the back of his mind; it felt like something asking to be known, or remembered. It grew louder as the car raced for the turnoff, and then, when they were on the hill above Ireland's store, something clicked. Weigand thought that it must have clicked loudly enough for Mullins to hear it, but Mullins gave no sign. Mullins was merely looking around at the countryside, over which the shadows of trees were lengthening.

He did not seem to notice that, just before he swung the Buick through the gap in the wall which was the Norths' driveway, Weigand began to nod slowly to himself, and that his eyebrows drew together a little, until there was a line between them. If he had noticed these things, Mullins would have felt less perplexed, but Mullins was thinking about the chance for an old-fashioned, or two old-fashioneds from the Norths. Mullins' own brow cleared when he decided that the chances were good.

· 16 ·

Lieutenant Weigand pulled the Buick up beside the Norths' car on the lawn and stepped from it with an odd urgency still driving him; stepped from it expectantly, with an inner readiness for emergency. Curiously, he felt himself braced against an onslaught, against an instant demand for the full employment of his faculties. And nothing could have been more disconcerting than the peace which closed in around him—the peace of a crisp, early fall evening in the country, with light slanting from the west now across the lake, with smoke rising unhurriedly from the chimney of the Norths' cabin, with that tiny, restful whir of evening noises in the air. It did not even seem to be a lull before a storm; the atmosphere was innocent of premonition.

And as he stood for a moment, startled and oddly disappointed by this, the feeling of urgency left him. He experienced a sensation of being overprepared—of being ready for more life than there seemed to be. He found himself obscurely dynamic in a static world, and felt a little foolish. And afterward, when the matter of the murders at Lone Lake had been resolved, Weigand was apt to cite that feeling as an example of how, sometimes, hunches will leave one in the lurch just when they are most needed. There was never, he would tell the Norths, recalling that moment, a time when the need for instant action was more imperative or when the direction of that action was, in reality, more clearly apparent. But the hunch which might have supplied the voltage of action died suddenly away.

It had died and left only a ghost. The ghost accompanied Weigand as, with Mullins beside him, he walked toward the cabin. But Pete, emerging to observe arrival, apparently did not see the ghost. Pete rolled over and presented a white belly, inviting attention from two accepted friends. Lieutenant Heimrich opened the screen door of the North cabin and emerged, but did not present his belly. He looked at the arrivals gloomily, and accepted abstractedly an introduction to Detective Mullins.

"Well?" Weigand said.

"Nothing," Heimrich said. "Except that these lead soldiers I've got working for me let virtually everybody get away. The Hunt girl, Abel, Kennedy—even the Smith girl. They all just walked away, or rode away, or something." Heimrich snorted. "And now this Saunders guy, after staying around all day like a little man, has wandered off some- where," he continued, "and would any of my mounted policemen have noticed it?" The question was disgustedly rhetorical.

"I'll tell you, Weigand," he continued, riding his grievance, "the State Police fell apart when they quit using horses. With a trooper on a horse you could be sure, anyway, that the horse would have some sense. And now what have you got? Just a trooper on a motorcycle!"

Weigand was careful not to agree with him, suspecting that Heim- rich, in his present mood, would grow apoplectic in the face of agree- ment. Heimrich would, Weigand thought, explode in defense of the troopers at the faintest echo from without of this angry grumble from within. Just as I, Weigand thought, probably would defend Mullins. He watched Mullins fading, as well as his bulk permitted, into an obscurity from which he could escape to the Norths and their pre- sumptive rye.

"It's a hard place to watch," Weigand said, mildly. "Probably there's no harm done, in any case."

"Well—" said Heimrich. "It's a hell of a note, just the same. Did you work out anything in town?"

A few things, Weigand told him. Mullins disappeared within the cabin, and Mrs. North's voice was raised in greeting, as Weigand tersely recapitulated his day. He told of Jean Corbin's luncheon engagement, of Abel's telephone call and of the interview with Abel's secretary, of the substantiation of Mrs. Wilson's account of the expected inheritance. He sketched, lightly, his interview in the district attorney's office and said he had visited the apartments of both the murdered girls.

"Find anything?" Heimrich said.

"Well, no . . . " Weigand hesitated. "Nothing that seems to bear, anyway. I think, in fact, that we—"

He left the sentence in the air. Heimrich looked at him, studied his face.

"Come on," he said. "Out with it!"

Weigand shook his head.

"I may be onto something," he said. "That's true. It's as little a thing as you could imagine—maybe it means a lot, maybe it means nothing."

Heimrich told him not to be mysterious. Weigand shook his head.

"It's just something floating now," he said. "If I can tie it down, it's yours. Meanwhile, it's just a hunch."

"Oh," said Heimrich. "A hunch! I thought maybe you had something."

"No," Weigand said. "Just a hunch. Have you picked up anything?"

Heimrich nodded and said that, as a matter of fact, they had picked up one or two things. A technician had been called in to check the Corbin cabin and was preparing findings. After he had finished, a couple of troopers had proved that there was no body under the cabin floor. Heimrich looked a little sheepish as he reported this, but Weigand only nodded.

"And we found a boy with a piece of tubing," Heimrich added. Weigand's eyebrows went up. Heimrich said that he thought it hooked up, all right, but not that it got them anywhere.

Figuring that a tube of some sort might have been used to siphon gasoline from the tank of a car, which might have no drainage valve, to a can, Heimrich had sent troopers to likely places on a hunt. They had found a length of tubing in Van Horst's barn, but it had no odor of gasoline. On the other hand, Van Horst, shown the find, looked puzzled and said he thought he had had a longer piece. And then a trooper, checking the cabins on the far side of the lake, had seen two small boys playing on the shore with something and dropped over to investigate.

"On a hunch," Weigand pointed out, with a faint smile. Heimrich, following his line of thought, nodded.

What the boys had been playing with was a six-foot, more or less, length of rubber tubing. They had been busily filling it with lake water and emptying it again, apparently over each other, but there was still detectable a faint odor of gasoline.

The boys had advanced several theories to account for their possession, but had finally settled for what appeared to be the truth—that they had found it. They took the trooper who questioned them and showed him where they found it.

The place they indicated was a few feet off the back road which, circling the lake and passing close to the dam, wandered off uncertainly through the country, but finally joined the Patterson road, which connects with Route 22. The tubing had been thrown into some underbrush at the edge of a level clearing by the side of this road and the long grass in the clearing seemed to have been trampled. The trooper—"showing some sense for a change," Heimrich interjected—had lain flat on the grass, to the considerable amusement of the boys, and sniffed vigorously. He reported that gasoline had apparently been spilled there.

"And Van Horst thinks the tubing probably was cut off the length in his place," Heimrich said. "So we can figure that somebody cut it off when Van Horst wasn't around, as he generally isn't, and used it to siphon gas. Which gets us nowhere, because anybody here could have driven over there—at night or even in the daytime—and done the trick in a few minutes. No marks on the tubing, of course; no tire tracks, or anything helpful."

Weigand nodded. Still, he said, they might find out eventually that it fitted in. And if they did, it would be nice at the trial.

"Give the jury something to pass around," he pointed out. "Pleases juries, that does."

"Yeh?" said Heimrich. "What jury?"

Weigand admitted that, for the moment anyway, Heimrich had him there.

"So . . ." said Heimrich. "Well, I'll jog the boys up a little. Maybe somebody's come back. Although not that my Boy Scouts would have seen them, of course."

He went away, still disgruntled. Weigand joined the Norths and Mullins in the cabin. A small fire was burning on the hearth, and Mr. North, looking incongruously battered but not unhappy, was sitting on the couch. His functioning hand held a drink. So did Mullins' hand. Mrs. North set her drink down, and told Weigand he was just in time.

"Did you," she inquired, "ever see anything like that?" Her head indicated her husband. "Do you realize, he can't do a thing—not a thing? That I have to do everything—drinks and fire and get water. And that he just purrs?"

Everybody looked at Mr. North.

"Purr," Mrs. North commanded. Mr. North purred.

Mrs. North looked at Weigand and they both shook their heads.

"Did that sound like a purr to you?" Mrs. North asked, doubtfully. Weigand shook his head again.

"You purr," Mrs. North directed. Weigand purred.

"That," Mrs. North said, "was just plain snort. *This* is a purr." Mrs. North purred. Weigand and Mr. North looked at each other, and shook their heads.

"No," Mr. North said, "I'm afraid not. Close, perhaps, but not really purring. How about Mullins?"

Mullins looked abashed and consulted the lieutenant. "Purr," Weigand ordered. Mullins purred.

"I think," Mrs. North said, "that you'd better mix your own drink, Bill. And then dinner will be ready. Maybe we can purr better after dinner. And then you can tell us everything."

The fireplace fire grew brighter as the room darkened and Weigand, over a drink and then as they sat at the dinner table, told them "everything." He told them, in rather greater detail, all that he had told Heimrich. And he told them also, speaking slowly and with a good many pauses for the exact word, of Dorian Hunt's appearance at the Wilson apartment. When he had finished, his tone left the topic open.

"And," said Mrs. North, "that puzzled you. You being a man and everything."

"For 'everything' read 'policeman,'" Weigand said. "Don't you think it was puzzling?"

"Yes," Mr. North said, fishing awkwardly for a piece of meat with an unschooled left hand. "A very funny business. Damn!"

"You poor lamb," Mrs. North said. "I'll get it." She got it and, when Mr. North opened his mouth in pleased anticipation, popped it in. "There's nothing puzzling about it at all, only she's a woman."

"Granting," Mr. North said, and chewed, "gender, I still think it's puzzling. Not as puzzling as if it were a man, of course. Nothing is."

"What?" said Mrs. North. "Does that mean something?"

"Things that would be puzzling in a man aren't in a woman," Mr. North amplified. "That goes without saying."

Mrs. North looked at him suspiciously. He looked at her blandly.

"Anyway," Mrs. North said, obviously putting the matter away for another time, "it seems perfectly simple to me, considering everything. She wanted to get the picture."

"Well," Weigand said, "I don't see that you explain it, Pam. We knew she just wanted to get the picture, didn't we? And it's still puzzling, isn't it?"

"I think you and Jerry are outrageous," Mrs. North said. "Detective Mullins understands perfectly, don't you—" she hesitated—"Detective Mullins."

"No, ma'am," said Detective Mullins. "I guess the Loot will understand all right, though."

Detective Mullins, having thus transferred responsibility to its proper setting, helped himself to more meat.

"Men," said Mrs. North. She said it hopelessly. "All men," she amplified. Two men, thus reduced to an obviously unsavory microcosm, waited.

"It was her father," Mrs. North explained. "And everything she had been through. It left her—oh, upset, sensitive. And then this. A man could have been calm and reasonable, but to her things sort of swelled up, out of proportion. They do, with women—I don't know why. So when this came along and seemed, somehow, to connect up with that other bad time—well, she just had to do something. She had to keep the things from getting tangled, and keep her father out of it. Her father has always been very close to her, I imagine. And when there was all that trouble—well, her feeling became more than normally intense, and she magnified little things. Like the picture. So all she knew was that she had to get the picture, because it connected her father up with something else that was disturbing and frightening and—"

She looked at Mr. North and then at Weigand.

"Oh," she said. "You'd have to be a woman. Women. I know just how she felt. It was just the way a woman would feel." She looked swiftly at her husband. "Women are funny, Jerry," she said. "Didn't you know?"

"Yes," Jerry North said. "Only I didn't know *they* knew."

"That," Mrs. North said, "was very stupid of you. And that's the way it was with Dorian."

Weigand looked thoughtfully at the fire, pushing back his chair.

"I can't say you make it much clearer, Pam," he said. "Or much—safer."

His voice trailed off.

"I'm sorry," Mrs. North said. "It's clear to me, Bill. And safe."

There was a rather long pause.

"In a sense," Weigand said, then, "I feel as you do about it. That it was—well, call it an impulse; the impulse of a sensitive and imaginative person under strain. I can see it that way. But I can see it another way, too." He looked into the fire. "Being a policeman," he said. "Among other things.

"The trouble is," he went on after another moment, "is that once we accept irrationality, under circumstances like these, we accept anything. It becomes difficult to draw a line between little unreasonable things and big unreasonable things. I don't mean they are the same, or that there isn't a line. I don't mean that an impulse to get a picture, for example, isn't a tremendously different thing from an impulse to—well, kill. Different from inside, that is—different to the person concerned. But it is very difficult to draw that line from outside. And as a policeman, I have to."

He lighted a cigarette and sent the match twirling into a blue flame which wrapped itself around a log.

"We meet every day," he said, "people who appear, from outside, to be irrational. It may merely mean that their minds are quicker than ours—that they jump steps, in speech and in action. Inside, to themselves, they are completely rational. We meet emotional people who do things on impulse, and they are usually fine people—people we like. Interesting people. And then, if you are a policeman, you meet other people who look much the same, and act on impulses—and when they have an impulse to kill somebody, or set fire to a tenement, they act on that impulse, too."

"But that's silly," Mrs. North said. "Anybody can tell."

That, Weigand said, was true only under certain circumstances. If you knew an impulsive person really well, closely, you could eventually come close to predicting, not the course or extent of any individual impulse, but the general limits beyond which impulse couldn't go. Long acquaintance, affection, perhaps—with these things you could come to tell, accurately enough. But it was hard to tell while you were still looking on from outside.

Mrs. North smiled, very gently, at the "still." But nobody else noticed it.

"The trouble is," Weigand went on, "that murder, too, is always irrational. We talk about motives for murder, but there are no rational motives for murder. The hazard is always greater than any goal, unless you are immediately defending your life. Murder becomes possible only when a motive—an advantage to be gained, that is—swells up irrationally in the mind. Gets out of perspective. When the possible gain swells so that you cannot perceive the risk. You needn't be insane for it to do that, or much more emotionally—well, swept—than the average. It may merely catch you when your resources are weak. The gangster intentionally weakens his sense of danger before he kills, usually by using drugs. If you commonly yield to impulse, you may weaken resistance. Or, equally, you may not."

He stared into the fire. Subconsciously, he wondered why he was saying all this—what waiting period these words were filling.

"I suppose that all I'm saying is that a tendency to yield to impulse in any person is more or less what, as a policeman, I'm looking for among any given number of people who may have committed a crime," he said. "Particularly a murder. And—well, there you have it."

"No," Mrs. North said. "You're not thinking straight, Bill. There's something wrong in it. You're getting lost."

Weigand threw his cigarette into the fire and said maybe he was.

"As a matter of fact," he said, "I'm wool-gathering, for some reason. I'm—"

"You're talking about something merely because you want to talk about it," Mrs. North said. "Or—about somebody. Somebody your mind wants to hang onto, and worry about. Even when there isn't any cause. You're making an argument because it keeps you close to—all right, Bill, to Dorian Hunt. Did you know that, Bill?"

"Pam!" Mr. North's voice was warning. "You're talking nonsense, Pam."

"Am I, Bill?" Pam North insisted. "Do you want to say I'm talking nonsense, Bill? Maybe I am, you know."

"Sure," said Weigand. "Maybe you are, Pam." He shut thought out, made his voice lighter. "Anyway, Pam, not before children," he said. "Remember Mullins, Pamela. Remember Mullins."

"Oh," said Pam. "Mullins is all right, aren't you, Mullins?"

There was no answer.

"Mullins is asleep, I think," Mr. North said. "Anyway, he's gone over to the couch. He looks asleep."

They investigated. Mullins was asleep. Weigand woke him up and he said, "O.K., Loot."

"The mighty Mullins," Mrs. North said, pleased. "Fidelity. Even when asleep."

They lighted more lamps, and their brightness chased shadows, too, from Weigand's mind. A new briskness, also, was apparent in the Norths.

"All this to the side," Mrs. North said. "Are you getting places?"

Weigand looked at her with interest, and then nodded.

"As a matter of fact," he said, "I think I am. I think it's all in. And I think there's enough of it."

"But then—" Mrs. North said, and her husband, too, looked at Weigand expectantly. He did not answer directly, and they searched his face. "You know!" Mrs. North said. "And all this—all this *really* didn't count!"

"Well," Weigand said, "say I hope I know. I did want your reaction to Dorian's visit to the apartment. Forget the rest—say I was just talking, and put any reason to it you like. I want to check what I remember. About Blair, particularly. I think it may hang on that."

"Blair?" Mr. North said. "But he's in the hospital. Oh, yes, I forgot to tell you. They think he'll be all right. He recovered consciousness this afternoon for a little while, but not enough to be questioned. But by tomorrow—"

"Tomorrow?" Weigand said. "You're sure of that?"

"Why," Mr. North said, "I'm fairly sure. Somebody called up the hospital, I think—I believe it was that chap Kennedy. He stopped by to see how I was making out, and said something about it. But Heimrich would know, wouldn't he?"

Weigand's mind moved, now, with sudden swiftness, and there returned to it that odd feeling of urgency. Would Heimrich know?

He ought to know, certainly; there ought to have been a guard on Blair. But he wasn't sure that anybody had thought it worth while, or that Heimrich had wanted to spare the men to guard a man not expected to recover consciousness for a good many hours. But if he had, and if Heimrich did not know—

"Listen," he said, "tell me this. You were both here when we questioned Blair. He told us what he did Saturday, from the time he got up until we found Helen Wilson's body. I want you, together, to go over that and tell me what you remember—without my prompting. I want to see if your memories check mine. So—they got up Saturday morning, and—"

Working it out together, checking each other, adding memories of what Blair had said out of the order of their saying, the Norths pieced it together. Weigand shook his head. They pieced it together again, adding a point here and there. And then, at one moment of Blair's day, Weigand suddenly stopped them, and had them check it again. They agreed.

"All right," Weigand said. "We remember it the same way.* And of course you see it, now?"

The Norths looked at each other. Each waited for the other. And finally, puzzled, they shook their heads.

"Well," Lieutenant Weigand said, and it could not be denied that he appeared to be a little gratified, "I think it's there, all right. Just keep looking."

And then he sobered.

"Only," he said, "if I'm right, it isn't over. If I'm right, the murderer—" He stood up, suddenly. "Mullins!" he said. His tone was all policeman. "Come on, Mullins. We're going places."

---

* If the reader, also, wishes to refresh his memory of John Blair's statement he may read on pages 85 to 87 all that Lieutenant Weigand and Mr. and Mrs. North heard.

• 17 •

MONDAY
8:43 P.M. TO 8:54 P.M.

The New York Central's Chatham express, out of Grand Central at 7:19, due at Brewster at 8:38, was five minutes late that Monday evening. At 8:43 it stopped impatiently at the Brewster station and puffed eagerly to be on its way. Dorian Hunt's heels clicked on the steel floor of the smoking-car vestibule and an official hand on her elbow gave her unneeded assistance. Her heels clicked on the concrete of the station's floor and beyond the doors on the station's entrance platform. Then they stopped clicking, while Dorian looked around.

The Wilson car, which Arthur Kennedy had promised to drive in to meet the 8:38, was not among the little group of waiting cars. He hadn't, apparently, been able to get through Lieutenant Heimrich's loosely drawn cordon of troopers; possibly, Dorian thought, there had been a stricter watch since her easy escape of the morning. Which meant a taxicab.

But there were no taxicabs, either. She looked where there should be taxicabs, and one of the small town's anomalous guides offered counsel.

"They're all out, miss," he said. "Brisco said to tell anybody there'd be a car back in about twenty minutes, or half an hour, maybe. They've all gone to meet."

This cryptic report meant to Dorian Hunt merely that there was no cab available. It meant to the young man in the leather windbreaker that all of the cars owned, and operated, by Salvatore Brisco were at the moment engaged in getting people from the countryside, so that they might be brought to the station for the 9:12 to New York. Miss Hunt nodded and asked the young man in the windbreaker if he could think of anything. He thought, wrinkling his brow to prove it, and shook his head.

"Guess not, miss," he said. "Just have to wait."

Dorian Hunt hesitated a moment. Brewster offered few enticements to the becalmed traveler. Then she appeared to make up her mind and her heels clicked off. They clicked across the street and along the sidewalk which climbed the hill to the left. Then they clicked up the sidewalk of the steeper grade to the right and on toward a square brick building of which Brewster was proud—a new brick building, with a semicircular drive in front and a neat plaque at the right of the door announcing: "Brewster Memorial Hospital." The plaque did not reveal what was memorialized.

Miss Hunt, who might be combining sympathy with necessity, went into the Brewster Memorial Hospital.

Dr. James Harlan Abel got off a rear car of the 8:38 when it arrived at 8:43. He saw the slight, swiftly moving figure of Dorian Hunt under the station lights and his uninterested eyes lingered a moment. Then his path diverged. He crossed the street diagonally and walked down Main Street, looking at the parked cars. He found the car he was looking for and his eyes flicked the empty driving seat. He halted in front of the car he had chosen, and for the first time hesitated. Then his shoulders moved in the slightest of shrugs. He walked on along Main Street and turned into a drugstore a few doors farther along. He sat at the soda-fountain and ordered a Coca-Cola, and as he drank it kept his eyes on the street.

At 8:48, the Wilsons' middle-aged Pontiac nosed into a parking space in front of the station and Arthur Kennedy jumped out, leaving a long-faced, rather bitter-looking girl on the seat. He went into the station quickly, looked at the clock, compared it with his watch and said, "Damn." Then he went back to the car. It was empty and he made a sound of vexation. He looked around and apparently did not find what he was looking for. He crossed the street and went into a bar.

Thelma Smith, walking quickly away from the station, continued along Main Street until she came to the First National store. She went in.

Mrs. James Harlan Abel came out of the notion store next to the garage on the opposite side of Main Street and crossed to her car. She looked at her watch and shook her head, looked toward the station and got into the car. She sat first in the seat next the driver's; then she moved across under the wheel. Then she lighted a cigarette and leaned back.

Hardie Saunders parked his new LaSalle carefully and got out of it unhurriedly. He looked at his watch, which assured him that it was 8:49. It was not quite dark, he noticed—not quite the dark of full night. But the dusk was heavy. Saunders lighted a cigarette, tossed the match aside, and sauntered off.

A State trooper, unobtrusive in civilian clothes, watched the arrival of the 8:38, which had come in at 8:43. He saw Dorian Hunt turn up the hill and James Harlan Abel cross the street. He watched the arrival of the Wilson car and raised his eyebrows over Thelma Smith's sudden departure from it while Kennedy was in the station. He observed Kennedy when he returned and, after Kennedy crossed to the saloon, strolled after him. Some time earlier, he had noted the arrival in Brewster of Mrs. Abel and seen her park diagonally in Main Street.

The trooper entered the barroom, saw Kennedy at the far end with a glass in front of him, and paid no attention to him.

"Guess I'll have a beer, Jim," the trooper told the bartender. "How's tricks?"

It still lacked a few minutes of nine o'clock when the trooper finished his beer. He tossed a coin across the bar, and looked down it toward Kennedy. Kennedy wasn't there. The trooper looked puzzled for a moment, and the bartender, watching him, intercepted his gaze. The bartender nodded his head toward a door at the rear of the barroom, and enlightenment appeared on the trooper's features. He told Jim he'd be seeing him, and to be good, and walked without hurry toward the door. On the steps outside he stood reflectively for a moment, lighting a cigarette. Then he made up his mind, in pantomime, and turned to the right. He walked up the hill, in the direction Dorian Hunt had taken.

John Blair, his head heavily bandaged, slept restlessly. At 8:45, a nurse opened the door of his room and crossed softly to the hospital bed. She looked down at Blair for a moment and then nodded. She crossed to the window and opened it a few inches from the bottom and stood for a moment looking down into the grounds below. The hospital stood in a little park, and in building it the contractor had been careful not to injure, more than was necessary, the trees which grew around it. Hence, although the hospital was brightly new, its surroundings were comfortably aged. The tree nearest the window could tell of fifty years.

It was dark under the trees, but then it was almost dark everywhere. Cool air came in through the partly opened window. The nurse, rustling faintly in stiff white, turned from the window to the bed again, and looked down at the sleeping man. He seemed to be quieter, now; the doctors said he would almost certainly recover. The nurse nodded at him approvingly, and then looked at the watch on her wrist. She nodded approvingly at the watch and went out of the room, closing the door behind her. She walked on rubber heels down the long hall toward the diet kitchen.

John Blair had strange dreams. He was sitting in the sun, which fell on him warmingly. Then a shadow formed and lay across his body, shutting off the sun. He could not understand what made the shadow, which lay so heavily on him. It was a strange shadow. It had pressure, weight. It crept over him and grew heavier. It was not a shadow, but a dark substance, impalpable but oppressive. It moved over his face and it was hard to breathe through the heavily pressing shadow.

"I'm dreaming," John Blair thought. "I've got to wake up! I've got to wake up!"

He tried to push sleep aside, to tear it away. Sleep was pressing too heavily on him—on his body, on his head. Didn't sleep know that his head was hurt? Didn't—?

John Blair's hands came up from his sides, fighting against the pressure on his head.

The nurse finished her cup of coffee in the diet kitchen, and doused in the dregs the coal of an unauthorized cigarette. Well, it was time to get back to the patient.

Lieutenant Weigand glanced at his watch as, with a willing but bemused Mullins behind him, he went out of the Norths' door toward his car. The buzz of urgency was back in Weigand's mind, but now there was no vagueness in it. Weigand knew where he was going—at 8:44 o'clock by his watch—and he was going fast. Mullins was still pulling the car door closed behind him, the Norths were watching, with surprise on their faces, from the doorway, when the wheels of Weigand's car spun a moment on damp grass as the clutch went in. The car jumped backward and turned to face the gap in the wall. Almost before it stopped, the wheels spun again and it leaped for the road. A car coming up the road from the right checked suddenly, and skidded on the crowned macadam as the Buick's siren snarled.

The Buick was doing fifty on the narrow road as it passed Ireland's store and swerved on the road toward Brewster, nine miles away. Two minutes later, with a mile and three-quarters of twisting, high-crowned road behind it, the Buick went into Route 22 without slackening, and then the speedometer needle swung around to seventy within a quarter-mile.

"Things happening, Loot?" Mullins inquired, mildly.

"Maybe," Weigand said. "Blair, I'm afraid."

Mullins gripped the side of the door as they went at sixty-five around a wide curve to the right.

"These babies move right along, don't they, Loot?" he said, pleased. And, with a smile of content on his face, he felt under his coat and loosened a police automatic in a shoulder holster. Feeling the grip in his hands, Mullins nodded in approval. Weigand caught the expression, and a smile cut momentarily across his face.

"Happy, Mullins?" he asked.

"It's all right with me, Loot," Mullins said. "We'll fix 'em."

The Buick went around a curve to the left at seventy.

The Norths looked at each other, and Mr. North shook his head.

"I guess I don't get it," he said. "What came over Bill, do you think?"

Mrs. North shook her head, puzzled.

"He saw something," she said. "That's the way he acts when he sees something. Only, what?"

Mr. North shook his head.

"Think!" Mrs. North said. "You think, and I'll think. Something about Blair."

"All right," Mr. North said. "You think. What about Blair?"

It was something, Mrs. North said, that they had all missed the first time; something they remembered but did not understand.

"We told him," she said. "And now we don't know. Quick—what did Blair do Saturday?"

"Well," Mr. North said, "he and Saunders got up and had breakfast and then Saunders went to Brewster and Blair came over to play tennis. Wasn't that it? I don't see anything in that, do you?"

Mrs. North looked at that, and shook her head.

"No," she said. "I don't think I do. Was it something about breakfast?"

Mr. North shook his head. He said he didn't see it.

"Or tennis?" Mrs. North said. "Or later—wait a minute." Her forehead wrinkled. "Wait a minute," she repeated. "Something's coming! Maybe it was—oh!"

"Oh! What?" Mr. North said. "If you are—"

"Come on, Jerry!" Mrs. North said. "Oh, we were stupid! Come on!" She was running toward their car.

"Listen," Mr. North called. "What the—"

"Come on, if you're coming!" Mrs. North called, yanking open the car door. "Don't just *stand* there!"

Mr. North found himself crossing the yard. He was crossing it at a trot, which hurt both his head and his arm, and he was trying to get sense out of Mrs. North as he trotted.

"Come *on!*" Mrs. North said. "It will all be over if we dawdle."

"What will be over?" Mr. North said, in breathless confusion, and braced himself with his sound arm against the dashboard as the car lurched backward, with protest from the gears.

"Everything!" Mrs. North said. "The murderer. Everything!"

The car jumped through the gap in the wall, and Mr. North shivered convulsively. He loosened his hold to run the only available hand desperately through his hair, and then grabbed for the dashboard again as the car swerved at Ireland's.

"Oh," said Mrs. North, "I don't see how we could have been so foolish! And he's afraid about Blair, of course. His being conscious again and everything, and the murderer remembering and all. And Blair knowing!"

Mr. North's words were devout. His tone was otherwise.

"If you would only—" he said, turning in his seat so that he could get a grip on the inner handle of the door.

"It was empty!" Mrs. North said. "Only it wasn't! And we missed it."

Mr. North shook his head and started to reply. Then he decided that he would not, under these rather appalling circumstances, distract Pam North from the business which rested, so hazardously, in her hands. If they ever stopped; if ever this demoniac progress through the approaching night was ended, and if they were still alive, he would speak to her sternly. But now—

And then something in her last words echoed in Mr. North's mind and his grip on the doorhandle relaxed and he stared unseeingly ahead. So *that* was it! He sighed, and shook his head.

"I must be stupider than anybody else," he told himself, resentfully. "Than anybody else in the world."

He looked at Mrs. North's intent profile. It was lucky, he thought, that he had married so well. He reached down and turned on the lights, which Mrs. North had, in some incomprehensible fashion, been getting along without. He would finally tell her how well her mind worked, he thought. If they lived, of course.

• 18 •

MONDAY
8:51 P.M. TO 9:22 P.M.

Nurse Frazier stood up, half-heartedly flicked the front of her uniform to dislodge crumbs, and glanced at her watch with instinct for time which comes to those who live by schedule. She walked from the diet kitchen toward Room 41, which was occupied by John Blair, and she was in no particular hurry, nor did any sense of urgency trouble her mind. She moved abstractedly, tasting the flavor of coffee and cigarette which clung to her mouth. Midway of the corridor a door opened and Nurse Carlin came out. Nurse Frazier and Nurse Carlin stopped.

"Always," said Nurse Carlin, with resigned bitterness, "he's having a sinking spell. But always. And ringing his head off."

Nurse Frazier nodded understandingly.

"And isn't," she said. "Patients!" Her tone was hopeless about patients. "The things they want!" she amplified. "Thank heaven, Forty-one's still out."

"Well," said Nurse Carlin, as a parting acknowledgment. She went on down the hall. Nurse Frazier shook her head, over patients apparently, and went on to Room 41. She hesitated a moment outside the room and heard a small sound, as of someone stirring. It sounded as if Forty-

171

one might be waking up, in which case she must notify the resident, who was, she had heard, obligated immediately to notify the police. Nurse Frazier opened the door. She stood rigid a moment before she began to scream.

In that moment the dark figure which was standing at the head of Forty-one's bed, bending down and doing something with its hands, turned a face which was a blur only less dark. The hands did not move for that instant, the body was stilled in the moment of action, set in the muscular pattern of energy, but without energy. Then the scream of Nurse Frazier shattered the moment. The scream, high, with sheer astonishment and terror mingled, floated back down the corridor. It caught Nurse Carlin as she neared the diet kitchen door and stopped her as if it were a noose hurled suddenly, and tightened, over her moving body. She whirled, with a hand up in a subconscious gesture of repulsion.

The scream echoed down the corridor and down the stairs. At its first sound a nurse at the information desk, seated, a record book before her, moved convulsively. Her pen scratched against the paper, caught and splattered ink in a shiver of arrested motion. Dr. Adams heard it in his office behind the information enclosure, and started to his feet, and as it came again threw the door open and came out running. Bending over a patient on the lower floor, a nurse and an interne, talking in whispers beside a bed, heard it more faintly and threw up their heads and listened and stared at each other. Then it came again and the interne broke for the door.

And in Room 41, the dark figure which had been bending over John Blair turned as the scream began and was at the window in one long movement. The figure was going through the window to the fire-escape outside as the scream still sounded down the corridor, and by the time Nurse Frazier had dashed light into the room with a frantic flick of a hand, there was no figure in sight, but there was a hurried, scrambling sound on the fire-escape. Nurse Frazier ran to the bed.

Her scream still seemed hanging in the air—she could hear it still in her ears—as she snatched at the pillow which covered Blair's head, and against which one of his lifted hands was spread motionless, palm up. Her quick fingers searched for a pulse as there was the slap of running feet in the corridor. Nurse Carlin stood in the doorway, a hand at her breast.

"What—?!" she said. "What is it?"

"The doctor!" Nurse Frazier told her, the voice tense and high-pitched, and the fingers still seeking the pulse, the eyes intent on the suffused, motionless face. "They tried to smother him!"

Dr. Adams was there, then, brushing the nurse aside, calling for adrenaline, working swiftly, and both nurses moved deftly, with professional sureness, at his direction. It was not until the racing interne burst into the room that there was time for anyone to lean from the window at which Nurse Frazier pointed. By then there was nothing moving in the shadows of the park, under the heavy foliage of the trees. But so fragile had been this moment that the interne, leaning from the window, could hear the scuffle of feet in the gravel at the side of the hospital, as someone ran, hard, around the building toward the semicircular drive in front, where cars could be, if they were backed a few feet onto the turf, parked in darkness.

Then the interne reached for the telephone on the bed table and, as Adams and the nurses worked, blowing on the spark of life which might still remain in the body of John Blair, shouted into the transmitter.

The girl at the information desk shouted for a porter who should be somewhere near and, at almost the same moment, spun the dial of an outside telephone to the police number. Her cry for the porter passed beyond the doors and reached the slim young woman in green, with a yellow ornament on a green hat, just as she stepped down from the last step onto the arching drive in front.

She stood with a foot on the drive and the other motionless on the step behind her, and turned her head. Then, at another sound, her head moved back again and she was staring at the corner of the hospital. Gravel crunched under running feet and Dorian Hunt raised both hands, with the fists clenched, toward her breasts. She was standing so, as if frozen, when the runner came around the corner of the hospital and at the sight of her checked for a moment and threw up one hand as if to hide a face. But the gesture was only an involuntary one, without meaning, because a gasp from the girl at the steps had told its story.

"No!" Dorian said. "Oh—no!"

And then, from the menace in the runner's movements, Dorian Hunt started to run. She ran across the semicircle toward the road which wound down the hill from the hospital. But there was a rush from her right and, as she dodged, an ankle turned under her. She seemed to be falling a long time and then, almost before her outstretched, protecting hands touched the ground, she was snatched up again. She struggled against a strength that was greater than hers—a strength that, irresistibly, bore her backward and to the side. She tried to cry out, but a hand clamped heavily on her mouth, bruising her lips.

William Weigand, driving as Mullins had never seen him drive before, took eight minutes to do the nine miles, part of it on a winding, crowned road, that separated the camp from the traffic light set where Brewster's Main Street stemmed off to the right from Route 22. It was 8:52 when, reaching that intersection, he wasted half a minute behind cars which had stopped dutifully on red, and were confused when the siren sounded behind them. A woman in the car at the head of the line trembled violently, looked anxiously at the red light, put her car convulsively in gear and stalled her motor. She was still stalled when the Buick, twisting out of line with siren speaking in anger, whirled around her.

From Route 22, Brewster's Main Street goes, with a moderate twist or two and usually with cars parked where they will do the most harm, up a grade. When it straightens out in the business center it is wider, but there cars are parked diagonally—a position which increases curb capacity, to merchantly satisfaction, but makes progress slow. Not even a siren can move such cars, or widen the narrow lane they leave open in the center.

Weigand could have avoided the loss of more than a minute here, to his subsequent peace of mind, if he had known Brewster better. If he had known Brewster better, he would have turned up a diagonal street which climbed the hill to his right a couple of hundred yards up Main

Street from the traffic light. This would have taken him up the hill, and to a street above which paralleled Main Street and from which the winding road which dead-ended at the hospital led, after another few hundred yards, off to the right. But the diagonal street was not an inviting one unless one knew its habits, and did not very earnestly promise to lead anywhere. So Weigand ignored it.

And even after he gained the business center, and was stymied for seconds behind a grocery supply-truck, he might have reached the hospital more quickly if he had taken the first turning to the right, and gone up a hill which was about as nearly perpendicular as a street can be without shedding its pavement. That would have led him straight to the parallel street on the higher level, and left only a short jog to the left before reaching Hospital Road. But Weigand, driving by instinct and completely sure only that the hospital was on the hilltop, passed that turning and took the second. This led up a less precipitate grade, ended in the same parallel highway, and required a jog to the right for Hospital Road.

The Buick's motor spoke angrily as, shifting down for greater speed, Weigand forced it up the hill. At the top there was a moment's pause before the right jog became clear. And then, as they swung to the right, they were in time only to glimpse the twin tail-lights of a car which turned sharply down at the next corner, headed for Main Street. Weigand knew there was trouble ahead, and that there was trouble dropping recklessly down the almost perpendicular street toward Main, only after he had guided the Buick into Hospital Road. He went on, then, up the twisting road, with the motor shrill under the hood.

It was half instinct which made Weigand, once he attained the maneuvering space offered by the hospital's entrance plaza, swing the Buick in a circle, so that it headed out again. Then the car stopped and swayed on its springs as the handbrake went on and Weigand was out while it was still swaying. As he ran toward the hospital doors they parted violently, and a State trooper emerged as if propelled. A man in not very clean white clothes emerged after him.

"Yes," Weigand said. "Let's have it!"

The trooper had been running, and his reply was gasped.

"Tried to get Blair!" he said. "Pillow—smothered. Ran around—car. There was a girl here!"

"Girl?" Weigand snapped. "What girl?"

The trooper shook his head.

"Asking for Blair," he said. "Just before the nurse screamed. Must have come out here about the time he ran around the building. Looks like he got her, too!"

"Blair?" Weigand asked.

It tumbled out. Somebody had tried to smother Blair with a pillow. Man or woman, the nurse didn't know. He had got into the room, and out of it, by means of the fire-escape and the window. The information girl had heard the sound of a motor starting a few seconds after she had called for the porter, but before the porter—"that's him," the trooper said, pointing to the man in white—came. It was the information nurse who had told them about the girl who had, just as trouble broke loose, stepped out of the hospital.

It clicked in Weigand's mind. The car they had seen, moving fast, turning toward Main Street. He was running toward his own car, calling back over his shoulder—calling anxiously, because of an unreasoning fear.

"The girl!" he shouted. "What did she have on?"

The car was in motion before the answer, relayed out from the nurse at the information desk, came back. The trooper ran toward the car as it moved away.

"Sort of a green dress!" he shouted. "Green dress!"

Weigand heard, and the car leaped under them. It burst from Hospital Road into the street; its tires shrieked as it swung left, leaning on the outside springs. It went down the steep street toward Main and the siren howled a warning ahead. Then Weigand had, with everything seeming to hang on it, to play a hunch. The car he was after—if he was right in being after it—might as easily have turned either way. Weigand turned left, and the note of the siren lifted.

The traffic light at the intersection of Route 22 and Main Street was red against them when the Norths came riotously down the hill toward

Brewster. The brake pedal dropped under Mrs. North's foot and the car swerved a little, with tire rubber wailing against the pavement. Mr. North caught himself with his left hand against the windshield and said, "Say!"

"Light!" Mrs. North said. "Oh."

The "Oh" signalized Mrs. North's realization, for not the first time, that a green arrow under the red light indicated approval of a right turn. Still moving faster than its driver realized, the Norths' car swung wide into Main Street and Mr. North emitted a wordless shout. Mrs. North threw the wheel over hard and the car shivered convulsively. But the car coming down Main Street toward Route 22, and also swinging wide for a right-turn, did not falter. Fenders grazed and there was a clatter as rear bumpers jabbed together and apart.

"Damn!" said Mrs. North. "Where does he—"

"Him!" Mr. North shouted, shouting her down, and shouting grammar down. "He's getting away!"

Mr. North was leaning back over the seat, staring out through the little window in the rear.

The car which had grazed them was completing its swing into 22, heading toward New York.

"And somebody else!" Mr. North said. "A girl, I think."

Mrs. North acted. Her still moving car stopped in a lurch. It backed violently toward 22, swinging to face after the fleeing car. A car which had started around the curve behind the Norths' scuttled profanely for safety. Mrs. North, in a state of magnificent concentration on other matters, paid no attention. Before her car had stopped backing, it was jammed ahead again. Mr. North thought in a fury, and yelled.

His shout went off in her ear, and Mrs. North's head swung to meet it. Her eyes were faintly glazed with purpose. Mr. North was forcing open the door beside him, struggling awkwardly with his left hand.

"Weigand!" Mr. North said. "Guide!"

He almost tumbled to the pavement, and slammed the door. Mrs. North was nodding inside, and the car was moving again.

"Not too close!" Mr. North yelled. "Just keep him in sight!"

Mrs. North was nodding again, and continued to nod as the car leaped forward. Mr. North stood for a moment, dazed by rapidity. He stood in the cone of light which poured from the bottom of the hanging traffic signal and splattered on the concrete in a wide puddle.

Then he was waving his injured arm and the sling which held it as lights from a car racing down Main Street glared in his eyes. He heard the protest of tires on macadam; saw the approaching car slow lurchingly. It hesitated beside him and the rear door nearest snapped open. Mr. North dodged it and fell in.

"Right!" Mr. North told Weigand, at the wheel. "Toward town. Pam's after them!"

Weigand said nothing, but the gears jerked the Buick into motion. Mullins, half turned in the seat beside the lieutenant, looked at Mr. North wonderingly.

"Jeez!" said Mullins. "How'd *you* get here?"

Detective Mullins' mind pursued action at a dogtrot.

"Pam doped it and we came," Mr. North explained. "We hit the surface twice, I think, coming in from camp."

He paused to worry. He thought of Pam going riotously around curves, driving, at last, as fast as she had always wanted to drive. He shuddered and cursed his arm.

"You're sure we're right?" Weigand asked over his shoulder, without turning.

"Yes," Mr. North said. "We both saw them—or I did, anyway." It occurred to him that he had no idea what Pam had seen. "Is it Dorian, too?"

"Yes," said Weigand. The word came flat and hard from his lips, like a sliver of glass. And then, driving at better than sixty around the curves over a stretch of crowned black road, Weigand began to curse. The words seemed to be blown back by the motion of the car. Mr. North had never heard Weigand's voice so hard, or his words so hard. They straightened out on concrete, and the speedometer needle jumped. Far ahead there were the twin tail-lights of a car, and they ought, Mr. North thought, to be coming nearer. But they kept their distance.

"Pam is in front of those lights," Mr. North thought, desperately. He shuddered at the thought, and leaned forward to look at the Buick's speedometer. The needle was at seventy-five, and climbing. "Please, God," Mr. North prayed, "slow her down!"

It is three miles, more or a little less, from the traffic light in Brewster to the first fork off Route 22 toward New York. There 22, relapsing again into pock-marked macadam, swings to the left and uphill. That is the way Sunday motorists take for New York. But to the right, N.Y. 100 bears off, in shining new concrete, and that is the road of the experienced. The Buick topped the last hill before the fork and roared down it, the siren crying for a clear way through the narrow underpass below the New York Central's tracks.

They jogged through the underpass at better than forty, and eighty had been more safe a minute before. They had done the three miles in a little over two minutes. Ahead, splitting the fork, were the twin tail-lights of a stopped car.

"Pam!" Weigand said, before Mr. North could be sure. "Good girl!"

The Buick shuddered to a stop beside the Norths' car, but there was no more finality in its halt than in a bird's when the bird banks for a moment against a puff of air. Weigand leaned from the window and Mr. North wrenched at the door.

"Right!" Mrs. North said. "At any rate—the only lights I've seen. They've got to be the ones!"

Mr. North was scrambling out, banging his injured arm.

"With you!" he gasped to his wife. "They'll go first."

They had already gone first, cutting in a half-turn and moving west on 100 as if some gigantic rubber band had snapped them into flight. Mr. North was back beside Mrs. North as their car began to back, and swing to follow.

"Take it easier, Pam," Mr. North pleaded. "You've done swell." The tail-lights of Weigand's Buick were points far up the road. "Let the cops do it, Pam," Mr. North urged. "Umph!" Mr. North was flattened against the seat as the car started.

Weigand, at the wheel of the charging Buick, was no longer swearing. The helpless rage which had prompted that had been submerged by a desperate hope. They were chasing tiny red lights through the night, on a frantic guess. There was nothing ahead—but there was something ahead! A point of light, tiny and red, flickered up the road.

"There!" Mullins promised, and pointed. His pointing hand withdrew under his coat, and its fingers gripped the butt of his service gun.

"No," Weigand said. "Somebody else—or one's out. There'll have to be two lights."

But by then it was already apparent that the single light was not the one they chased. It grew closer rapidly; the driver of that car was not fleeing anything. The siren whined a warning and the car ahead swerved, bumping on the shoulder. The Buick went past a little coupe, and a white face peering from a window. Ahead, then, there were no lights at all. Then, beyond a hill, there was a white glare mounting, and again the siren challenged. The lights of the car coming toward them flared in their eyes, dropped as a dimmer switch was clicked. The siren whirred impatient thanks. Now there was really nothing ahead, except white road under the Buick's questing lights.

But the road was hilly, and looped over the country. You could see a mile ahead, perhaps, before a hill hid the road or a curve sent lights plunging momentarily against trees. There was only hope, and wild chances to be taken.

It was safer to do what he was doing at night than in daylight, Weigand found himself thinking as they cut close in to the left side of the road around a curve. Approaching lights flared warning against the sky; against trees and bushes. Even around curves—

They straightened out and swayed. Mullins twisted to look behind. They had gone more than a mile on a straightaway before he saw what he was looking for. Lights from the following car plunged around the curve.

"The Norths are coming, Loot," he said. "Coming like blazes."

Weigand nodded, his eyes searching the road. Far ahead two tiny red spots glimmered briefly and vanished. Weigand's foot sank on the accelerator, until it met rubbery resistance. This model was supposed to do better than a hundred, and now was the time to find out. The speed increased slowly, and now the siren was still. There was only the high, shrill note of the motor, and the singing of the tires on pavement. The headlights ate into the darkness, which seemed to have grown lighter.

"Moon, Loot," Mullins said. His voice was snatched from his mouth, tossed on the torrent of air from the open window beside him. Mullins looked back over his shoulder. There was a big moon coming over a hill. Mullins thought it was mighty pretty.

The headlights bounced on the blackness of tree-trunks and the car bumped against the brakes. Then it rolled free again, around a curve on the inside. Ahead the road was straight, and now there was no doubt of the two tail-lights ahead. They must be moving very fast, but the Buick was gaining—gaining a little, snatching fractions of miles, parts of seconds, out of the distance between.

"That's them, Loot," Mullins promised.

"Right!" Weigand said. "I think so."

The speedometer needle climbed again. Well, it would better eighty, anyway, Weigand thought. He would write a testimonial—if they came through. "Police Lieutenant William Weigand, forced to use the utmost speed in pursuing a desperate—" Hell! Pursuing a girl in a green dress; pursuing a dream he had never had before at better than eighty on a narrow road full of curves and hills; pursuing two tiny spots of red that dipped, now, out of sight over a hill; climbed into sight again beyond and now vanished utterly.

They curved down a long hill toward a traffic blinker. Beyond the blinker, 100 became Pines Bridge Road, twisting on the lips of reservoirs, through soldierly woods of evergreen, planted by the distant city; green sentinels of the water supply. And nobody—nobody in the world, with the world after him—could go very fast on that road and keep the road. But maybe—

The siren hurled its warning at a car which crept across the intersection ahead. The car jumped. The Buick thundered through. The pavement was older, here; the Buick chattered over it. And the curves were sharper.

The moon looked into the Buick, and two faces peered ahead. They were both white, but all faces are white in moonlight. Mullins clutched the side of the door, as they went around another curve which would have forced him into Weigand.

"There!" he shouted.

The car ahead was losing speed. The tail-lights were closer, now. The Buick was losing speed, too, but not so much.

It was somewhere along here this morning that a girl in a green dress had cried out "Curve!" Weigand thought—somewhere a little farther on. He had told her about policemen, then, and how protective policemen were; how everywhere one goes, there are policemen, actual or ideal, to stand on guard. He took a curve so fast that the car skidded a little on dry pavement. The fleeing red lights were much closer, now.

They were not more than half a mile ahead on the next straightaway—the straightaway which ended, Weigand suddenly remembered, in the curve which had been the real curve of Dorian's warning. The car ahead was plunging at it, and now the fan of its headlights on the road were clear, and the red lights seemed to leap nearer as the fleeing driver, with the lights of pursuit bright in his mirror, slowed for the curve. And then—

There was a sudden flash of light within the car in front. It was on—off!

"What the—?!" Mullins said. And then his voice went up, hoarsely. "Watch out!" he shouted. "Jeez!"

The brakes of Weigand's car closed on spinning brake-drums. The Buick checked dizzily, but neither Weigand nor Mullins had thought for their own peril.

The car ahead lurched. It twisted as if for the curve, and then there was a roar of sound—of thin metal buckling, of tires dragging sideways on concrete, incongruously among them the sudden blare of the car's horn. Then the car was reeling off the road to crash against safety cables strung tight at the road's edge. It hung there for a moment and then, rather slowly as it seemed, toppled over. The lights of the Buick blazed on the car as Weigand skidded it to a stop.

There was movement in the wrecked car, which lay on its right side.

The door in front seemed to fall from its hinges and a man stood in the light, raising a hand to shield his face. Then, heavily, the man began to run.

"Get him!" Weigand said. He and Mullins spilled from the car, Mullins with his gun out. Weigand heard it speak, but it was not speaking in his world. He ran toward the wreck and as he ran there was a sudden puff of fire on the ground beside it. The fire leaped, as he ran, to the side of the car—it was hungry, hurrying fire. Then, as he covered the last few feet, more lights swooped down on them, and he heard tires jamming to a stop on concrete. But that was not in his world, either.

His world was hard, resisting. He tore at it with his hands, and felt blood on them from jagged metal. Then the twisted steering column which barred him from the motionless figure of Dorian Hunt came away in his hands. And then flames were hot on his back and side, and his hands were leaving dark splotches on the shoulders of a green dress. For a moment his world hung in flames and effort; then Dorian seemed light in his hands and there was a swishing sound somewhere. He lifted Dorian clear and had her in his arms and clear of the wreck, on which flames licked eagerly. Mr. North, a fire-extinguisher perilously in his sound arm, hugged against him, was playing a foamy stream on the flames, which turned on it resentfully and hissed and fell away.

"Got him!" Mullins was yelling from a little way off, and there was a dark blur of Mullins in the moonlight and a darker blur at Mullins' feet. "Leg!"

Then Weigand was bending over Dorian Hunt, and half supporting her in his arms, and Mrs. North was kneeling on the other side, with fingers on Dorian's wrist.

"All right, Bill," Pam North was saying. "She's just knocked out, I think."

Then Dorian's eyes were open and she was looking up at Weigand and saying, in a far-away voice,

"Hello, policeman."

Then the eyes focused, suddenly.

"Did you get him?" Dorian said. "Did you get him, Bill?"

Weigand nodded.

"Oh," he said, remembering something a long way off. "Yes, we got him. We got Saunders for you."

The eyes looking up at him seemed to change.

"For me?" Dorian said, but she said it softly, with a kind of tenderness and a kind of amusement. "Thank you, Bill. It—well, I see what you mean about policemen, Bill." Then her eyes closed, and there was a kind of inertness in the body he held. Weigand looked at Mrs. North, with a desperate question in his eyes. But Mrs. North smiled.

"She's just fainted, you idiot," Mrs. North said. "Can't a girl faint? Under such fine circumstances?"

Weigand looked at her anxiously, but she seemed very sure. And when, at Mrs. North's direction, he laid Dorian flat on the ground—"so she can get blood in her head," Mrs. North explained—Dorian lay white and still only a few moments and then opened her eyes again. Seeing Weigand still bending over her, she smiled a very little and closed her eyes again. Weigand decided it was all right.

• 19 •

MONDAY
10 P.M. TO MIDNIGHT

Mrs. North laid logs on the fire in the cabin and poured kerosene over them. After a moment of rising white smoke, the kerosene puffed into flame and the logs caught. They sat for a moment watching the fire, with only dim lamps burning. They looked battered. Dorian Hunt, her green dress stained dark at the shoulders, snagged and pinned up at the side, leaned back against cushions on the couch. She was pale and quiet, and the light made a dark shadow of the bluish swelling on her left temple.

Weigand's hands were bound in white, and he used the fingers awkwardly with his cigarette, and one side of his face was reddened by the flames which had touched it for a moment. Mr. North sat with his injured arm swung across his chest and adhesive holding a pad of white on his damaged head. Only Mrs. North and Mullins of the five were unscarred, and Mullins, sitting in a shadow, was half asleep. For a time nobody said anything, and then Weigand said, with a kind of sigh, that it was over.

"He kept talking about it all the time," Dorian said, then. "All the time after he grabbed me and we started, he kept talking." She thought about it. "It was dreadful," she said. "He seemed—oh, I don't know—proud. Until he realized that somebody was chasing us."

She stopped and looked at the fire.

"He was going to kill me, you know," she said. "Just like that. He said it very calmly and logically—that he had to kill me because I had seen him after he had killed Blair. Saw him running away."

"And he hadn't killed Blair," Weigand said. "Again he hadn't killed Blair. Blair will outlive him, the chances are. But it was close."

"Was it?" Mrs. North said. "Very close?"

Weigand nodded, and lifted his drink. He said it was close enough.

"A matter of a few seconds," he said. "Blair was almost done. But they brought him around. He'll live to testify." He hesitated, and turned to Dorian.

"Dorian—" he said. He said her name slowly, as if waiting for contradiction. She said, "Yes, Bill?"

"I see it up to a point," he said. "You had gone to ask about Blair? Right? And you saw Saunders running away and he realized you had recognized him. And he'd had experience with hasty killings, and was going to make sure, so he took you along for—for later action. Right?"

Dorian nodded to each "Right?"

"But what made him wreck the car?" Weigand asked. "He was going all right until then. We were gaining, but he was going all right. What happened?"

"A match," Dorian said. "I remembered the curve and thought it was a good time."

"What kind of a match?" Mrs. North wanted to know. Dorian said just an ordinary match. She said it was this way:

"If we got away," she said, "he would kill me. He made that clear enough. If I grabbed the wheel, or anything, I would wreck us, only maybe I wouldn't be strong enough. But if I could wreck the car, at the right time, I'd have a chance—a better chance. So I said would it be all right if I smoked, and when he said yes I lit a match."

"Oh," Weigand said. "I see."

Mrs. North said that maybe he did, but she didn't. "A match?"

"I held it up toward his eyes quickly," Dorian said. "Just when we were coming to the curve I lighted it and held it up. And it blinded him; it—"

"The flare," Weigand amplified, when she hesitated. "The sudden light in relative darkness. The eyes contract like a cat's, and when the light goes out, you're blind for an instant. Can't see the road. So you smash."

"Oh," Mrs. North said, "of course. I've done it. Only not smashed up."

Mr. North made sounds from his chair.

"You've done it to me," he said. "Not meaning to. And we've almost smashed."

"Listen—" Mrs. North said. She felt the others looking at her, and saw Weigand smiling. "Oh," she said. "All right. For the moment." She thought. "There seems to be a lot of fire in this case," she said. "Gasoline in fireplaces. Matches. Cars burning." She looked at their fire. "And it looks so peaceful," she said.

"What I don't get," Dorian said, after a moment, "is how you all knew. I didn't know—I was groping. But all three of you did know, didn't you?"

"Well," Mr. North said. "Yes, eventually. Bill first. Then Pam. I trailed pretty badly."

"But how?" Dorian wanted to know. The Norths looked at Weigand. It was, Weigand said, merely through falling for a slip. Saunders' slip.

"He should have got rid of the kerosene," Weigand explained. "Or bought some more. But he had just the wrong amount."

Dorian shook her head.

"I'm too tired to think," she said. "Tell me. Was it something somebody said?"

Weigand nodded.

"Something Blair said," he explained. "Something he said and almost got killed for. He said he had gone back to the house that evening and built a fire."

Dorian thought it over, and shook her head again. Weigand told her that it was only a tip, of course; not evidence. But they had evidence. Motive—that was clear. Saunders knew that Jean Corbin was trying to get the Quench account away from him. That was the only account he had that amounted to anything; on it his agency stood or fell, and with it his professional future. He knew that the account was apt to go if she stayed alive, because of Fillmore's confidence in her ability. With Jean dead, Saunders believed the account would be safe. He was probably right in that belief. And there were subsidiary motives. She had helped edge him out of Bell, Halpern & Bell. She had been his mistress, and left him bitter and with hurt feelings. But chiefly it was the Quench account.

"That much we knew," Weigand said. "But there were others with motives, both for killing Jean and for killing Helen Wilson. And it was impossible to pin down opportunity very exactly. Too many people had it. We were in the position of being able to prove if we knew, but not knowing. Then we remembered what Blair had said."

"Speak for yourself, Bill," Pam North said. "Not Jerry and me." She paused. "I," she said. "No, me. Do not speak for me."

"About building the fire," Dorian prompted.

Weigand nodded.

"We knew," he said, "or we assumed, that the person who had arranged the trap for Jean had done certain things. He had taken two cans, one full of gasoline, to her cabin. He had emptied the kerosene from the can in her cabin into the empty can, and filled her can with gasoline. That left him with an empty can and a can of kerosene. The natural thing, and as it seemed to the murderer—Saunders as it turned out—the safest thing, was simply to put the kerosene back in his own cabin and use it up. So—"

"But Saunders himself, not thinking it would help us, let out the fact that Saturday morning, Blair had used up the last drop of kerosene in their cabin in filling the lamps. And then Blair let out—"

"*That he built a fire that evening!*" Mrs. North said, not waiting. "And since everybody builds fire with kerosene—"

"But do they?" Dorian said. "And couldn't he have bought it?"

"I said it wasn't evidence," Weigand explained. "It merely was a moral certainty—it won't be any use in court. Defense counsel will ask just that. But we knew that it was a universal custom at the camp to build fires with kerosene. We knew that Marvin doesn't sell kindling, and nobody has ever indicated that any of the campers went out into the brush and cut their own. So we could assume, for our own purposes, not a jury's, that if Blair built a fire Saturday evening he built it by pouring kerosene on the logs. Only where did the kerosene come from?"

He held up his hand.

"Your second question," he said. "Yes. Well, we checked with Ireland yesterday. We got a list of people who had bought kerosene the day before. And neither Saunders' nor Blair's name was on the list. Somewhere else? It was possible. But why, since everybody did buy kerosene from Ireland, since it was the most convenient place, and since it must have been a habit—why? Defense counsel will call this thin. But it goes back to this—habits don't break themselves. If they are broken, they are broken by human decision, *for a purpose*. And what innocent purpose did anyone have, on Saturday, for breaking a habit about the purchase of kerosene?"

He waited. Nobody said anything.

"Right," he said. "That was the way it looked to me. So now, what have we got?" He paused, but not for an answer. "We've got the unexplained appearance of a two-gallon can of kerosene in the Saunders-Blair cabin between sometime Saturday morning and late Saturday evening. And what do we want? Somebody who has picked up two gallons of kerosene in that period without buying it or borrowing it— somebody who has just found it! Blair or Saunders."

He took a drink.

"Both have motives," he pointed out. "Saunders has a strong motive for killing Jean Corbin. Blair has a strong motive for killing Helen Wilson, and possibly, a slighter motive for killing Jean. But when we think it over, we know it's Saunders."

Mrs. North shook her head at that.

"When Blair gets slugged, you mean," she said.

"No," Weigand told her, "when we think it over. Unless we want to base it on Blair's very slight motive for killing Jean—the apparent fact that she was ditching him for somebody else. Because, if we base our deduction on the appearance of the kerosene in the cabin between Saturday morning and Saturday evening, we know the killing of Jean is the primary crime. She's not killed because she knows something about the murder of Helen Wilson, because the trap is set for her *before* Helen is murdered. In logical sequence, Jean was murdered earlier than Helen, not later, in spite of the fact that Helen died first. So—Helen was killed because she knew something about Jean's murder before it happened. Say she—"

"She stumbled in on him, he said," Dorian told them. "He had just finished setting his trap Saturday afternoon—when he had gone to put on the stew—when she came in. She was going to leave a tennis shirt for Jean, you remember. She was surprised to see him there, because she knew Hardie and Jean weren't friendly. He put her off, somehow—he didn't say how. But he knew that, when the gasoline exploded—he thought it would explode, he said—Helen would remember that he had been there, and tell the police. He was very calm about it. 'So of course I had to kill her,' he said. 'You see that, don't you?' Then he said: 'Just as I have to kill you.' "

Dorian shivered momentarily.

"It was—" she said, and hesitated. "Awful," she finished. It was a lame word, but it did not feel lame in the half-darkened cabin.

"Right," Weigand said. "It had to be that way. So he killed her, slipping away for a moment from the Fullers' party, after he had seen her go out. Then he acted, I think, very much like an innocent person all day yesterday—or did, so far as we could tell. But he undoubtedly listened to us when we were questioning everyone?" Weigand looked at Dorian for confirmation. "Yes," she said. "He said he listened."

"He heard nothing of importance," Weigand went on, "until we were questioning Blair. Then he heard Blair tell about building the fire, remembered he had told us that the can had been emptied, and decided that Blair might put two and two together or that we might and have Blair as a witness. So he decided it would be necessary to kill Blair. And Blair—well, Blair apparently made it easy for him. We'll find out when Blair is better. But we can assume, meanwhile, that one of two things happened: Blair thought it over himself and grew suspicious and watched Saunders. Saunders decided to take back the empty can he had borrowed from the cabin, and Blair followed him and gave himself away and got slugged. Or, perhaps Blair didn't put two and two together, but guessed where the empty can had come from and, because he thought we suspected him, kept watch on the unoccupied cabin on the chance the can might be put back. The first is more likely."

He seemed to have finished. Then he started to speak again, and did not form the words which seemed ready to be formed. The three who were awake waited. Mullins snored gently.

"And the rest?" Mrs. North said, finally. "The others with motives?" Weigand shrugged, his hands spreading.

"Nothing," he said. "Things that cropped up, as they always do in a murder case. It is like—well, it is as if a side of a house falls away, or is bombed away. You see all the rooms people have been living in; you see all sorts of things you aren't asking to see; pry into things that don't have bearing. Only, in a murder case, one of those rooms may have the secret, so you have to open them all up. It is—trying for the people whose secrets come out undeservedly. But that is the way it works."

His voice sounded tired. He finished his drink and stared into the fire. Mrs. North, after a moment, fixed him a new drink—she mixed them all new drinks. Her movement awakened Mullins, who looked interested. He got a drink.

"So Helen was just—unlucky," Dorian said, after a time. "She stumbled into it—into death."

Weigand's head agreed.

"Stumbled," he said. "And died out of turn. Yes."

"And Saunders will be convicted?" Mr. North said, from where he nursed his arm and his glass.

"Oh, yes," Weigand said. "I should think so. Certainly."

He was abstracted, staring into the fire. He felt tired, and oddly dispirited. They finished their drinks. After a time, Dorian stirred, and then stood up. Even in weariness, Weigand thought, watching her, her movements flowed into one another.

"I'd better go home," Dorian said. Her voice was weary, too; her tone abstracted. "To the Wilsons', that is—until tomorrow. It—" She stood in front of the fire, and did not finish whatever she had started to say.

"Why not here?" Mrs. North said. "There's no reason for you to go."

Dorian shook her head.

"Things," she said. "All my things—"

She started toward the door. Weigand stood up, suddenly.

"May I walk down with you?" he said. The words came quickly, hurriedly. Dorian looked at him and smiled and said she would be very glad—He followed her through the door, into the moonlight. They walked down the path, needing no other light than the moon's. Her face was very white in the moonlight.

"You're tired," he said. He said it as if the words were part of something more which was not to be said. She did not answer, directly. But then she spoke.

"About the picture," she said. "I'm sorry about that—but—" She hesitated. "I was nervous," she said. "Frightened. And it seemed to me that I had to keep the picture hidden, because it would bring Father into it. Can you understand?"

"Yes," Weigand said. "It doesn't seem odd."

"I knew she had it," Dorian said, after a little. "She showed it to me, once—oh, a long time after the trial and everything, when we were friends. You see—Father sent it to her *after* the trial, to show that he didn't—"

"Yes," Weigand said. "I see how it was."

They walked on. She was a little ahead as they went along the path past Van Horst's and came to the Wilson house. The porch was sprayed with moonlight falling through trees. Weigand stopped suddenly at the foot of the porch steps, and Dorian went up them and then turned to face him. There was a pattern of leaves on her dress, but her face was clear in the light.

"Well—" Weigand said. The word hung in the air, as he looked at her.

"Well?" she echoed, and there was the beginning of a smile on her white face. "It's been—strange, hasn't it?"

"Yes," Weigand said. "I wish—" He did not say what he wished. He merely kept on looking at her. His gaze did not seem to make her rest-less; the smile which had come upon her lips clung to them. She wait-ed, he thought, for him to go on. But she was not disturbed that he did not go on. They stood so for rather a long time before, finally, she spoke.

"Well," she said, "goodnight—policeman."

There was something in her saying of the word which made it a dif-ferent word. She held out her hand and he took it and still looked into her face. The smile was still there.

And when he went away, after a moment, the smile somehow went along. After a little the smile was very bright in his mind, and he could hear her voice softly. When he got back to the Norths' he felt fine, and full of conversation, and Mrs. North looked at him interestedly. Mr. North, however, said that one thing about the country was that nobody ever got any sleep.

THE END